# MEREDITH'S GOLD

The peaceful existence of the Arizona town of Mountain Peak is cruelly shattered by the arrival of a bunch of outlaws, led by the unspeakable killer John Bannock. By murder and intimidation, Bannock quickly takes over the town ... but for what purpose? The townsfolk turn to the one person who might possibly save them: Randle Meredith, an urbane Eastern gentleman – until, that is, somebody crosses him. Meredith sets out to discover why Bannock should have targeted their town, and soon there are no holds barred in what becomes a personal duel between Meredith and Bannock.

# MEREDITH'S GOLD

# MEREDITH'S GOLD

*by*

Philip Harbottle

**Dales Large Print Books**
Long Preston, North Yorkshire,
BD23 4ND, England.

**British Library Cataloguing in Publication Data.**

Harbottle, Philip
    Meredith's gold.

A catalogue record of this book is
available from the British Library

    ISBN   1-84262-414-8 pbk

First published in Great Britain 2004 by Robert Hale Limited

Copyright © Philip Harbottle 2004

Cover illustration © Prieto by arrangement with
Norma Editorial S.A.

The right of Philip Harbottle to be identified as the author of
this work has been asserted by him in accordance with the
Copyright, Designs and Patents Act, 1988

Published in Large Print 2005 by arrangement with
Robert Hale Ltd.

Dales Large Print is an imprint of Library Magna Books Ltd.

Printed and bound in Great Britain by
T.J. (International) Ltd., Cornwall, PL28 8RW

*For E. C. Tubb*

# 1

## TAKEOVER

For several minutes, the travel-stained giant on the massive sorrel had been peering into the valley below him. His black suit was covered in trail dust, and his rough-hewn good looks were marred by dirt and stubble. His china blue-eyes squinted in the long bars of evening sunlight; then he hipped round in his saddle.

'Well, fellers, it looks good enough from where I'm sittin',' he commented finally. His five mounted companions, all of them every bit as saddle-weary as himself, looked at each other and nodded.

'Yeah,' one of them responded. 'I reckon that down yonder we might lie doggo for months without anybody comin' a-lookin' for us. And even if they do...' He patted the six-gun strapped down to his thigh.

'What I can't quite figure, Jack,' a second man remarked, 'is why you chose a dump like this?'

'That's because you never use what little brains you've got!' the big man retorted.

'Hell, Jack, there's plenty of hick towns around this district – but there ain't many as lousy as Mountain Peak! Why pick this one?'

'I got my reasons,' the big fellow replied. 'If you don't like the way I do things, that's just too bad! I can always git along by myself, remember – which is probably more than you critters could do!'

The big fellow grinned at the sour looks directed towards him and then he gazed down again into the valley at the town of Mountain Peak.

From the high vantage point of the rimrock, it looked like a toy town. In a wide circle about it, covering many miles up the verdant sides of the valley, were the small squares of ranches and their big corrals. Mountain Peak was prosperous and yet sleepy, basking day after day in the torrid Arizona sun, a town with a stormy past whose inhabitants were looking forward to a more peaceful future. They didn't know it, but their chances of that had vanished when the big fellow and his cohorts had appeared on the rimrock.

'You'd better leave me to do all the talkin' – and the shootin' if need be. I've got my own ways of doin' things and I don't want any of you jiggers ballin' things up. Right, let's go!' The big man nudged his spurs and started a sweeping canter down the valley side, his cohorts following on behind him in a cloud of dust.

The lower they went the more they descended into the shadows of the gigantic, impersonal mountains. By the time they had reached the main street of the ramshackle town, the brief twilight had fallen and the kerosene lamps were alight atop the board-walks.

At the far end of the churned-up, rutted, main highway the big fellow drew rein. His bright blue eyes darted quickly from a general store to a tin tabernacle, an assayer's, then to a sheriff's office, and finally encompassed the town's livery stable, sundry dwellings, and the Painted Lady saloon from which light was streaming in an inviting fan. From inside came the sound of a decidedly tin-pan orchestra and the blur of voices.

'Even worse than I thought,' commented the earlier grumbler. 'Stoppin' in this place is like bein' buried alive.'

'Better than bein' buried dead, Charlie,' one of the other men pointed out. 'It's still a hide-out, ain't it?'

11

The big fellow spat casually into the dust. 'OK, it's time fur a drink – and leave all the talkin' to me.'

He ambled his horse forward until he had reached the Painted Lady. He dropped from the saddle, slipped the reins on the tie rack, and strode up the steps to the batwings. Thrusting inside the tobacco-fumed den, he stopped and appraised the scene, his eyes narrowing critically.

People glanced once, then looked away. A trail-stained puncher, even if he was a stranger, was nothing unusual. For the big fellow, too, the scene was no different to any other in a hick town: there was the same assortment of tables with their customers in the shape of cattlemen, half-breeds, Mexicans, painted women, ranch women, and plain housewives. The scrape and squawk of the orchestra, the rattle of poker chips, the clink of bottles and glasses, the inaudible conversation wove into a blur of sound.

Jerking his head to his comrades, the big man strode across to the bar-counter.

'Double whiskey – and quick!' he told the barkeep. 'You jiggers can look after yourselves,' he added.

As though he wished to be dissociated from his companions, he picked up his drink and tossed it off; then he flipped money down on to the beer-slopped counter. He studied the scene through the back-bar mirrors. Presently his gaze singled out a broad-shouldered, lean-faced man in a black Stetson, with a star on his shirt pocket.

'When I give the word,' the big fellow said, gazing in front of him as he spoke, 'you all know what to do. Any man who panics will get the blasted floor blown from under him.'

The men to his right passed the word on to each other and continued with their drinking. Then the big fellow turned casually and looked straight across at the sheriff

'Hey, you! Come over here! I reckon it's time we had a word.'

The sheriff, obviously surprised at the authority in the voice, glanced up from watching a poker game, his eyes slit in suspicion.

'Suppose I don't feel like comin'? I'm not used to bein' ordered about by guys I don't even know.'

'You leery, Sheriff?'

That did it. The sheriff tightened his lips and walked towards the bar-counter, his right hand resting casually on the butt of his gun. It was as he closely considered the big fellow that he gave a start.

'Say, you're John Bannock!' he exclaimed. 'That mug of yours is on every reward-dodger between here and Caradoc City, and has been for months! Wanted dead or alive for robbery and murder–'

'Right,' the big fellow agreed tautly, and suddenly his guns were in his hands – and not only in his. At his one brief word, his five cohorts had their weapons levelled too, covering everybody in the room.

Sheriff Curtis was not the kind of man to be easily frightened. 'You've got your gall, haven't you?' he asked. 'Wanted in three States and now you come walkin' in here and pick on me – the very man who can, and will, run you in!'

John Bannock grinned crookedly, then spat on the sawdust-covered floor.

'I singled you out for one reason only, Tin Badge – you're runnin' the law around this dump. The setup's pretty simple: I'm hidin' out with my boys here, see? It ain't likely the law will ever reach into a backwoods town like this. I guess most of you don't even know what a marshal looks like.'

'They get around here sometimes,' the sheriff answered. ''Specially when I tip 'em off! You don't suppose I'm goin' to let you walk out of here?'

'You ain't takin' me in, Tin Badge. I haven't finished tellin' you yet why I picked on you. It was to take your job from you, see?'

Sheriff Curtis's hand tightened a little on his gun, but by no other sign did he betray his awareness of danger.

'In plain words, Tin Badge, I'm takin' over the town,' John Bannock explained blandly. 'With my boys, all of us faster on the draw than any of you mugs, it's a natch. And since you're hell-bent on givin' us away, I don't intend to let you!'

'You aimin' to try shooting me?' the sheriff asked grimly. 'You hold life pretty cheap.'

'Sure I do – and I aim to shoot you right now!'

The habitués of the Painted Lady had seen plenty of fights and gunplay during its history, but never a murder so cold-blooded as that which followed. Without giving the sheriff a second to draw, Bannock fired twice with both guns. Curtis stiffened, his hand sliding to his gun butt.

He stared stupidly for a moment and then dropped at the base of the bar counter, his face in the sawdust, his hand sending a cuspidor wheeling lopsidedly away from him. It came to rest with a clang against a nearby table.

The outlaw swung and looked about him, prepared for whatever might happen following his brutality. He saw tense, grim faces but nothing more. No man present was ready to shoot it out – not with six twin-gunned men who didn't give a damn for murder since their necks were already sold to the law if it ever caught up.

'I reckon that'll show you folks the general idea.' Bannock said at last, breaking the silence. 'I'm runnin' this town from here on, and if anybody opens his trap too wide about me or my boys bein' here, it'll be just too bad. You'll be watched, all of you, night and day, from somewhere you can't see.'

He waited awhile for the threat to sink in and then he continued, 'If you try and skip town to give information at Caradoc or Wilson City, you'll get lead blasted into you... Now, which of you mugs owns this dive?'

A tall, slender man in a tuxedo, with a white shirt front, came forward. He had an arrogant, bronzed face, but from his build was far more of an indoor man than one able to deal with this hardened desperado.

'I am,' he said, coming forward. 'What do you figure on doin' about it?'

16

'Keep your trap shut, feller; you'll find it safer.' Bannock looked him over sourly and then spat in the sawdust. 'A lily-white with the hands of a woman! OK, brother, you can continue to run this joint with no questions asked – 'cept that I get drinks free for me and my boys. Get it? There ain't any other demands – at present, leastways.'

'I should think not,' the saloon owner commented. 'As for free drinks, it depends how much you drink. I've just bought this joint, and aim to make a profit–'

'Shut up! I drink what I like, when I like, and as much as I like! Got that?'

The saloon owner shrugged. 'All right, Bannock, have it as you wish: you're on the right end of the hardware. I'm Bill Cranford. You'll get no trouble from me. Doesn't matter to me who runs the town – just as long as I'm left in peace.'

'So you can do all the gyppin' you like on the gamin' tables?' The outlaw gave a knowing grin. 'OK, somethin' else: who's the mayor? I suppose this cockeyed joint has got one?'

A stout man of late middle age, who had been watching the proceedings from beside an ornamental pillar, came forward. He had a dogged face and was plainly the type of man who would not be easily scared.

'Watch yourself, Mayor!' a 'puncher warned. 'That coyote is as blasted treacherous as a side-winder.'

Bannock wheeled, his face murderous.

'Any more from you, feller, and I'll let you have it,' he roared. 'No jigger calls me names more'n once and lives– And step on it, Mayor!'

The mayor said nothing. He kept on walking until he was within a few feet of the outlaw. Bannock studied him more closely. He was heavily built, with keen dark eyes, two chins, and a mouth like a rat-trap. A white Stetson was pushed up on to his greying hair.

'So you're the mayor,' Bannock commented. 'You one of those mayors who just sit on their backsides and let things take their course?'

'I get by. If you don't like the town, Bannock, we're not detaining you. We've little liking for murderers. I'm Mayor Taylor,' the stout man added. 'I'm also a cattle-dealer, owning the Blue-Circle ranch just out of town. I've other interests as well, but I reckon they ain't none of your business.' There was a general murmuring of assent.

The outlaw, his eyes glittering dangerously, caught the sound and hesitated.

'Better take it easy with this critter, Jack,' the nearest gunman whispered. 'The folks are all behind him.'

'OK, Mayor,' Bannock said, reflecting. 'I had to blot out the sheriff because he admitted he was hostile. With you I'm prepared to give you a chance to play ball.'

'Big of you,' the mayor commented drily. 'But don't be too sure that I'll do your bidding.'

'You will – or else, feller. And get one thing clear: you can't stay as mayor whilst I'm around, gettin' in my way, so there's only one answer. An election. Me against you. That fair enough?'

'You've got the guns,' the mayor responded. 'I can tell you right now, though, that the people here are quite satisfied with me as mayor and they'll simply vote me back into office.'

'Shut your trap!' the outlaw ordered viciously. 'Anyways, Mayor, that's the setup, and we'll hold the election soon as can be. I want to do some campaignin' first. If you've any sense you'll not stand as a candidate. Even if you're re-elected, I'll see to it that you won't have any power.'

'Then why hold an election?' Taylor asked.

'It just doesn't make sense.'

'It does to me: I want the people here to know that, whoever they get as mayor, it was done legal-like. For the time bein', until there is an election, you've no authority in this town. I'm takin' it on. Is there anybody here who'd like to argue?'

The men and women in the saloon looked at each other, murmured comments under their breath, but went no further. The outlaw waited for a moment or two and then nodded.

'OK. You're bein' sensible. You'll be told when to vote, and where. I'll take a look round first and decide where to live – probably at that hotel I saw down the street.'

'And of course you won't pay for your accommodation?' the mayor asked.

'Why should I? I never pay for anythin' when there's a certainty I can get it for nothin'. Anythin' you'd like to do about it?'

'Plenty, as a man who detests dishonesty – only as I said before you've got the hardware.'

'And don't you go forgettin' it, either! And,' the outlaw added, looking back at the assembly, 'in case any of you folks gits the idea of pluggin' me the moment I turn my back I'm always leavin' a man handy with his gun levelled. That's to warn you. Now, get this sheriff's body dumped on the mesa somewhere. You, Charlie,' he added, glancing at his right-hand man. 'Make sure that you bury it good and deep.'

'OK, Jack.'

Charlie nodded and moved forward. Effortlessly he hauled the dead sheriff on to his shoulder and left the saloon with his burden. The eyes of the men and women followed him and then moved back to Bannock. He smiled cynically.

'Later on, when the new mayor's elected, there'll be a new sheriff too,' he said. 'One of my own pickin'.'

There was a long, ominous silence. The outlaw looked about him and then added, 'That's all I have to say – for now. You boys,' – he glanced at his men –'stick around while I case the town. First job is to find the telegraph station and put it out of action. Then I'm pickin' a decent place where we can have all the comforts of home without payin' for 'em. Then I'll be back...'

The inhabitants of Mountain Peak were not any of them cowards, but on the other hand they were not foolhardy either. At the moment, the best way to stay healthy seemed to be to give the ruthless John Bannock his head. Whilst he could easily have been shot down by one or other of the men of the town, they refrained because they could never be sure but what an instant retaliation in lead might not spit at them from some hidden spot.

The outlaw's main intention seemed to be to run the town so he could keep himself safe there. After his initial depredations, he was not, as yet, instituting a reign of terror or upsetting anybody's business. The safest course seemed to be to let him have it.

In two days, one or other of his gunmen always on the watch, Bannock was quite firmly installed, with rooms for himself and his cohorts, free of charge, at the Mountain Hotel. His original intention of holding an election – and seeing that he won it – remained unchanged. He had even gone through the farce of having the local newspaper print a special section about the benefits which he could bring to the town when – not if – he became mayor.

Very few of the slow-thinking denizens of Mountain Peak grasped the fact that Bannock was holding the election purely to keep the people quiet and let them think they had a mayor rightfully and legally elected. To have shot down Taylor in cold blood so soon after the sheriff might have started something dangerous, and cut-throat though he might be, Bannock was not a fool. He was perfectly confident that his gunmen could make the populace vote for him whether they wanted or not.

As the days passed, people in the town and at the outlying ranches received visits from either Bannock himself or one of his gunmen, warning them that an election was impending and how they were to vote. They were surprised, and in some cases they even remonstrated – but before the gunmen departed, the potential voters knew exactly what they had to do, or else...

It was John Bannock himself who tackled the Slanting-F ranch, owned, so he had discovered in town, by Bart Meredith and his wife Jane, a newly married young couple. As such they should be more easily browbeaten into his way of thinking. So with complete assurance he rode into the yard of the Slanting-F and looked about him.

He saw only one person in the bright morning sunlight – a rotund individual in blue levis, forking straw from the yard into one of the outhouses. Bannock contemplated him for a moment, noting his enormous girth and semi–bald head; then he slipped from the saddle and ambled over to him.

'Hey, you! Where are the folks? Quit forkin' that muck for a minute and answer me!'

The man in overalls turned, surprised. He had a perfectly round face, triple-chinned, with a full-lipped mouth. Possibly he was sixty years of age, and built as massively as Falstaff. In general he looked childlike, with pink cheeks, white teeth, and round blue eyes of extraordinary innocence. In fact, just the kind of man Bannock felt he could enjoy slapping around.

'Where are the folks?' Bannock repeated curtly, the glint back in his eyes. 'I ain't got all day.'

'I was not aware that you were addressing me, sir,' the Goliath explained, as he came forward. 'Hence the hesitancy on my part.'

The outlaw stared at him. 'Who the hell are you? You talk like a goddam Limey...'

'I'm a Bostonian.'

'A New Englander!' Bannock sneered, cuffing up his hat. 'Ways off your territory, ain't you? What are you doin' out West?'

'My name is Randle Meredith, and I am foreman of this ranch, owned, for your information, by my son Bart and his wife.'

'OK, Fatty. Now shut your trap and git

24

those folks out here.'

'I'm sorry, but that is quite impossible,' Meredith smiled amiably. 'They left early this morning for Wilson City on business.'

'They did?' Bannock looked about him narrowly as if doubting the truth of the statement; then he shrugged. 'Well you can give your son a message – and it applies to you as well, Pop. There's an election comin' up, see? And only one person can possibly be mayor, and that's me.'

'Indeed, sir? Extraordinary.'

'Don't try to be blasted funny with me! I'm goin' to be mayor – extraordinary or other-wise,' Bannock continued emphatically.

Meredith gazed in some wonder, a half smile on his cushiony lips.

'That mug Taylor will be puttin' up too, but I don't aim to let him git away with it. If he should happen to win, a lot of people are goin' to taste hot lead. Savvy?'

Meredith considered the morning pens-ively.

'You are suggesting that you should have the votes – and nobody else?'

'Right! Vote for me – or else! Tell that to your son – and any other men workin' here – and git it well rammed down inside your own big belly too. I'll tell you when the election is. Be there – and vote for me, John Bannock. If you don't you'll have a lily on your chest afore you know it.'

'I have rather a dislike for lilies, on my chest or otherwise.' Meredith reflected, then: 'Forgive me, but if the issue is not the least in doubt I fail to see the purpose of an election at all–'

'I don't give a damn what you see. Just listen and do as you're told if you want to stay healthy. Otherwise I'll let some of the wind outa your flabby hide.'

Meredith said nothing, smiling faintly, his face a perfect full moon. The outlaw gave him a sour look and then rode off without so much as a backward glance.

'Remarkable,' Meredith murmured. 'One of those gentlemen of the West who considers himself tough by ignoring the benefits of a razor, talking out of the side of the mouth, and whipping a couple of guns from his belt. Remarkable!'

He reflected for a moment and then went up the ranch-house steps and into the living-room. Within it, a young man and woman were busily going through a bundle of accounts.

'Who was that character, Dad?' Bart Meredith asked, glancing up. 'I never saw him around here before. I was watching him through the window here. Was he looking for a job?'

'Quite the contrary. He told me his name is John Bannock and that he is putting up for the office of mayor in Mountain Peak. I had understood that Mayor Taylor was in charge – but apparently he has been deposed. It looks like gun-law again, I'm afraid – by no means an uncommon occurrence here-abouts.'

Bart's eyes sharpened and for a moment he ceased checking the accounts. He was an almost-handsome young man, black-haired, with dark-blue eyes. Though in limbs and figure he seemed a Westerner there was also something about him that testified to his Eastern origins, whence he had come to Arizona to battle with the life of a rancher and make himself worthy of the trust of the blonde girl he had made his wife.

'I thought gun-law had gone from this valley,' the girl said, frowning. She gave her father-in-law a questioning look. 'What's all this about, Randle? You've got the sort of look on your face that says you're keeping something back.'

'I've no wish to appear mysterious, my dear. Briefly, the facts are these–' and Meredith outlined his conversation with the outlaw.

'You actually mean he threatened violence if we didn't vote for him?' Bart demanded. 'The blasted nerve of it!'

'Quite, Son. However, I left him in doubt as to our intentions and took the liberty of telling him that you had both gone to Wilson City. I thought it preferable to be rid of him as swiftly and tactfully as possible.'

'Uh-huh,' Bart agreed, thinking. 'But I don't like the sound of this at all. I haven't been in Mountain Peak for the last fortnight, so I haven't heard what has been going on. From the look of things it would seem that this Bannock guy has taken over from Taylor...'

'And probably at the point of the gun, I imagine.'

'Wonder why?' Bart muttered. 'Jacob Taylor's as straight a mayor as Mountain Peak could wish for.'

'Naturally,' Meredith said, 'such a state of affairs cannot be allowed to continue. It is possible that the inhabitants around here, rather than argue the point, have agreed to do as Bannock has ordered. I'll be casting my vote for Mr Taylor. Were it not for the fact that he is also a candidate I would ignore this election fiasco altogether.'

'Tonight I'll go over to the Painted Lady and see what I can find out for myself,' Bart decided. 'I'm not having gunmen coming here and telling me what to do without knowing the reason why.'

'I'll come with you!' Jane said promptly, her blue eyes glinting. 'I'm getting pretty sick of being stuck around the spread, anyways.'

'No, Jane.' Bart shook his head. 'If gun-law has started in town again, and it looks as if it has, it isn't safe for you to be there. I'm better able to protect myself than you are. Dad here will see that you are OK whilst I'm gone. I couldn't leave you in better hands.'

'Thank you, Son.' Meredith murmured, and eyed the ceiling.

'But Bart, I want to–'

'Sorry, Jane. I'm going alone.'

The girl relaxed and sighed, giving her corpulent father-in-law a disappointed glance. To her surprise she saw his gaze lower and there was a gleam in his baby-blue eyes. It was a look she had seen before, so she tactfully dropped the matter and went on with the accounts.

# 2

## THIRD CANDIDATE

At sundown that evening Bart rode into town. Leaving his mare at the tie rail he strolled into the Painted Lady and looked about him. One or two of the men lounging at the tables nodded towards him familiarly. He nodded back.

That he still had the name of Dude amidst the community did not in the least bother him. He had already proved his worth as a man and a fighter, even if he was an Easterner who used judo technique when he found his gunplay was not swift enough.

At this hour, the saloon was not over-crowded, and presently he espied the man he wanted lounging comfortably against the bar and looking in his direction.

Many eyes followed Bart as he moved. At the bar he stopped and ordered a rye. When it had been given him he turned and looked the grim-faced outlaw up and down.

'You'll be Bannock, I suppose?' he asked.

'The guy who's putting up for mayor?'

'Yeah. Feel like doin' somethin' about it?'

'I'm not sure yet. That's why I decided to drop in here tonight and have a look at you.'

'Yeah? Like I was sort of cattle?'

'If you want it that way, yes.'

Bannock's jaw squared; then he relaxed again as Charlie, right behind him, pulled hard at his sleeve. The outlaw turned and snatched his arm free.

'What the hell's gotten into you?' he demanded fiercely.

'Take it easy, Jack,' Charlie insisted, in a hoarse whisper. 'This guy ain't like the rest of 'em. He's not a Westerner, for one thing, and he's plenty more brains than this dozy bunch. I've been hearin' things about him. He trucks around with a big-bellied guy everybody calls Homburg, and from what I can figure they're pretty hot stuff when it comes to makin' trouble.'

'Yeah?' Bannock reflected. 'The one with the big belly must have been the old guy I saw this mornin' at the Slantin'-F. He was just a windbag – nothin' to be scared of, any more than this critter is. There ain't no man breathin' who can best me in a showdown.'

Throughout this whispered conversation, which he could not overhear, Bart drank his rye and looked about him; then he contemplated Bannock again as the outlaw turned to face him directly.

'You'll be from the Slantin'-F, I suppose?' Bannock demanded. 'Where I was this mornin'?'

'Correct. Bart Meredith's the name. I believe you left some sort of crazy message with my father this morning – something about my father and I voting for you in a coming election?'

'For your benefit, feller, that message weren't crazy!' Bannock glared. 'You'd *better* vote for me, or else! I'm nominatin' myself as mayor against the former mayor – Taylor – and there ain't nothing illegal about doin' it, neither.'

'On what legal grounds was Taylor deposed?' Bart asked, and nodded to the barkeep for another rye.

'The legal ground of common-sense! Taylor knew better than to stay in office once I'd told him to git out. If he hadn't agreed to this election I'd have rubbed him out as I did Sheriff Curtis.'

A glint came into Bart's dark-blue eyes and he looked up sharply.

'So you took care of Curtis, did you?' Bart drank down his second rye and then leaned against the counter. 'As I figure this business you've blown into this town and instituted gun-law. You are having a mock election for mayor to make it look good and not antagonize the people too much. Those who don't vote for you will get rubbed out.'

'That's it. And if you want to stay healthy, feller, you'd better vote my way.'

Bart smiled cynically. 'Nobody tells me what to do, Bannock – and a no-good hoodlum like you least of all. For your information, not so very long ago we had a good deal of trouble in this valley, and I was more or less a prime mover in clearing it up. I learned one thing at that time: never give a crooked dealer an inch. Start in as you mean to go on, and blot him out! Not difficult making sure who's crooked and who isn't – you, for instance, are a wanted man. I remember now that I've seen your face stuck on bills up and down the territory, with a reward for you dead or alive.'

'That talk won't get you anywhere!' Bannock swore, fury making his tanned features even darker. His hand flashed to his gun – but Bart's empty rye glass followed it just as quickly. It splintered across the outlaw's knuckles, raising gashes and blood trickles. Bannock swore savagely and then realized

34

Bart's own gun was already trained on him.

'I'm not particularly fast with a gun,' Bart explained, shrugging, 'so I've worked out other strategies – such as taking you off guard with that rye glass a moment ago– Being Boston born and only coming here for my health a year ago, I've not grown up with a shooting iron in my hand. But I do know how to fire one, and unless you and your blasted gunnies get out of this town right away, and stay out, I'll let you have it. These folks are all witnesses – and they can say that I'm doing the community a service. They're peace-loving enough to accept your gun-law, but I'm not.'

'Like to have things your own way, do you?' Bannock sneered.

'I've enough to do with looking after my ranch, but I just won't tolerate outlaws, and–'

Bart broke off, starting back as something whistled like a snake close by his face. Before he could grasp what had happened a noose settled tightly round his gun wrist and jerked. The .45 flew out of his hand and clattered some distance away. Grimly he looked behind him.

One of Bannock's grinning satellites was coming forward, collecting the rope as he moved. He lifted the noose from Bart's wrist and eyed him cynically.

'You're right, dude,' he said briefly. 'You're sure not experienced, otherwise you'd watch all sides instead of just in front.'

'Now it's my turn to talk,' Bannock observed, his own gun in his hand and the men behind him ready for action. 'I thought when I'd rubbed out the sheriff that I'd removed all the opposition I was likely to git. Now I know different. Better start sayin' your prayers, feller– *Hell's bells!*' The outlaw broke off with a yelp of pain, as, with devastating suddenness, something struck him with vicious impact over the left eye.

He dropped his gun and clapped both hands to his face. His men looked about them dazedly, then wheeled round startled, as a bottle behind them splintered and flooded the counter with whiskey.

'I have you covered, gentlemen,' a voice remarked gravely. 'Drop your guns.'

For the first time the outlaws saw a ponderous figure with an enormous stomach and wide shoulders sitting at a nearby table. Formerly he had not been visible by reason of the gathered circle of men and women watching the proceedings.

Now the man rose and moved with extraordinary celerity on small feet, a .45 in his hand, a rather absurd black Homburg perched in the exact centre of his round head. That it was completely out of harmony with his check shirt, riding pants, and half-boots did not seem to worry him in the slightest.

'I shall not hesitate to shoot whichever one of you makes a suspicious move,' he said. 'And it will be straight to the heart. Now, kindly deposit your guns on the floor immediately, please.'

More astonished than anything else, the men obeyed, the hardware clattering to the sawdust-covered boards. Bannock kept one hand over his left eye and peered fiercely with the other one.

'Who the blue hell threw something at me?' he demanded. 'You, Fatty?'

Meredith inclined his head, a sardonic smile on his chubby face. 'You will remember me, I think? Randle Meredith at your service. If you don't, you may have cause to before I have finished with you.'

'Nice work, Dad,' Bart said, grinning, as he retrieved his gun. 'I didn't even know you were in the saloon, but thank heaven you were.'

'I know you instructed me to remain with your wife at the ranch, but having the feeling

37

that your inexperience might lead you into trouble I took the liberty of watching over you. Jane is at a table yonder, safely ensconced with Mr Cranford, the saloon owner.'

'Who the hell *is* this character?' asked Charlie, in wonder. 'A Homburg hat and ridin' pants – face like a newly washed kid. I ain't never seen anythin' like it! Anybody would think the guy was loco or somethin'!'

'As to my appearance,' Meredith commented, smiling, 'once seen never forgotten– But do not mistake my features for those of a buffoon. Nature has blessed me with the angelic smile of a cherub and the eyes of a child awakened in the night – but both those attributes, if one may call them such, are misleading.'

The men looked at each other dazedly, trying to sort out Meredith's Eastern grandiloquence.

'As to you, sir' – Meredith looked at the scowling Bannock – 'this was my weapon of attack.' Meredith reached into his shirt pocket and brought out a strong catapult. Bart stared at it and then laughed outright. Bannock glared with his sound eye and spluttered something to himself.

'A primitive weapon,' Meredith admitted,

shrugging, 'but I have found it remarkably efficient in these somewhat lawless parts. The sharp impact of a pebble on the anatomy is sometimes very helpful in distracting attention, particularly when it strikes the eye, or – if the occasion is propitious – the backside.'

'You might have damned well blinded me!' Bannock roared, removing his hand to reveal a sharp cut on his left eyebrow. 'I'll have the mark of that blasted stone on my face for the rest of my life!'

'I could have blinded you, yes.' For a moment Meredith's moonlike face was cold and expressionless. 'That, I confess, was my intention – but my aim was bad for the simple reason that it was hurried. It's time you realized that you are not dealing with what is popularly called a "pantie-waist".'

'You're tellin' us, Homburg!' an amused puncher commented.

There was a grim pause for a moment, Meredith with a gun rock-steady in his hand. With his fat jowelled smile he looked around the assembly, at Bart's levelled gun, then across to the slim figure of Jane as she pushed her way through the spectators. She hurried over to Bart's side and caught his arm.

'You hadn't real need to cause all this trouble, Bart,' she insisted. 'Fighting for the right is one thing, but you can't do it single-handed – or even double-handed if we include your father. Bannock and his men are killers, every one of them, and unless you have the support of the entire community behind you you're simply asking to commit suicide. Leave things be whilst you're still in one piece.'

Bannock looked at her. 'You said it! For a dame you've got plenty of sense.'

'Don't ever refer to madam as a dame,' Meredith snapped. 'It lowers the status of this lady to whom you have, referred. What's more, it fills me with an irrepressible desire to hit you on the nose!'

'Yeah? Just try it–'

In a matter of a split second things happened. Meredith dropped his gun to the floor and, knuckles clenched, he landed an extraordinary right-armed blow sideways. It was perfectly timed and hit the outlaw straight in the face. With a gasp he jolted back against the counter, caught his heel, then sat down in the sawdust with a thump.

Meredith smiled, and raised his Homburg hat momentarily. He retrieved his gun and held it as, his nose bleeding freely, Bannock got slowly on his feet, plain murder in his undamaged eye.

'Just give me the chance to git at you,' he whispered, balling his fists. 'One chance, and I'll tear you apart!'

'I'll be careful not to afford you any such advantage.'

'You might be enjoying yourself, Dad, but we're not getting anywhere,' Bart pointed out. 'It's a stalemate. These mugs won't get out and we can't force them to.'

'Yeah, you're hog-tied,' Bannock snarled.

'That being so,' Meredith agreed, glancing at Brad, 'I have a few suggestions to make. The upshot of everything seems to depend upon a forthcoming mayoral election. On the one hand we have Mr Taylor as candidate, and on the other Mr Bannock. He has made it clear that he will be displeased with those who do not vote for him. So I consider there should be yet another candidate and make it a three-cornered fight. Then the people, if they do not want Taylor, are not forced to vote for Bannock as an alternative. They can vote for the third party instead.'

'What third party? What in hell are you ravin' about, fatty?' the outlaw demanded savagely.

'I am referring to myself,' Meredith replied.

'I have for a long time fostered a certain desire to be mayor of this town. I am sure I could bring it inestimable benefits. Whilst having nothing against the methods of ex-Mayor Taylor, I have nevertheless noticed certain little details which require more finesse.'

'What in hell's finesse?' Charlie asked, his month gaping. 'The words this guy uses!'

'Shut up!' Bannock snarled at him. 'This guy's just a blasted windbag! I'll soon puncture him when I get the chance.'

'Maybe,' Meredith smiled. 'Your difficulty is, of course, getting the chance.'

'It's never occurred to me,' Bart said, musing, 'but come to think of it, it might be quite a good idea if you did become mayor, Dad. You'd make an excellent one.'

'You can forget this rubbish,' Bannock broke in angrily. 'Two candidates is enough for a burg of this size–'

'One – or else! Surely I do not have to remind you of your own threat?' Meredith said. 'Since that can hardly be called fair a third party is called for. Are you people agreed on that?' he asked, raising his voice and looking about him upon the assembly. 'Speak up – there's no need to be afraid of this owlhoot.'

'Yeah, sure.'

'Some of us don't want Taylor anyways, and we don't want that lowdown gun-hawk either.'

'By God, I'll...'

Bannock hesitated and then turned as Charlie caught at his arm and spoke in a whisper.

'Better do it, Jack. He's got you at the wrong end of a gun. If you want this stunt to look legal you have to agree to another candidate.'

'But if this damned pot-belly gets in—'

'So what if he does? It'll be a natch! He's only an over-grown kid with a big mouth. Just as good as havin' no mayor at all. We could still do pretty well just as we like. Take it easy. I'll gamble we ain't got nothin' to worry over.'

Bannock nodded and looked back at the blandly smiling Meredith.

'OK Homburg, if that's the way you want it. You're added to the nomination list. I don't agree with it – but nobody's goin' to say this election ain't fair.'

'I appreciate your sense of humour, sir,' Meredith commented. 'But I would add one proviso: if I am elected I shall be the legally constituted mayor of the town and you will

43

have lost your fight – and what is more you will then leave with your men as fast as possible! If you win, I shall have no further say in the matter. If Mr Taylor wins, the responsibility for being rid of you will be his.'

'OK,' the outlaw growled impatiently, dabbing at his eye and then his nose.

'For my part,' Bart said, 'I can't see the sense of this election business anyway. This guy's a wanted murderer. Why the devil do we have to play the game his way when all we need to do is inform the authorities?'

'A fair point, Son – but trying to inform the authorities might prove singularly difficult,' Meredith pointed out. 'I imagine that Mr Bannock has already foreseen that possibility.'

'Yeah, I sure have.'

'But if I should be elected mayor I shall have the authority, and will use it,' Meredith said. 'Mayor Taylor could have done the same, but presumably had not the courage. He preferred instead to stand down and let this farce take its course.'

'I'd no choice,' Taylor objected, from the further end of the room. 'And if you think the people will vote for you any more than for me, Meredith, you're crazy! Bannock's already told them what they'll get if they don't vote for him, and a gun's a darned sight more persuasive than a lot of words.'

Meredith considered the people for a moment, then said, 'If you allow yourselves to be stampeded into voting for this outlaw, my friends, you will institute a reign of terror which will finally drive you out of the territory. It cannot be otherwise with gun-law. If you vote for me, or Mr Taylor, you will show common sense and reap the benefit... Remember that. Now, Mr Bannock, have you decided when this election is to be?'

'Tomorrow,' the outlaw snapped. 'And if you think them fancy words of yours will make any difference to the result you're mighty mistaken, Homburg.'

'We shall see...' Meredith glanced at Bart and the girl. 'If you are ready to depart?' he asked, and motioned with his gun.

They nodded, backing towards the bat-wings. Meredith kept the gunmen covered until the last moment, and then, satisfied that the girl and Bart were on their horses, he went swiftly down the steps and leapt into the saddle of his powerful stallion. With a ponderous clomping of its big feet it set off up the high street, leaving a whirling cloud of dust settling behind it.

Back in the saloon Bannock made no

attempt to follow, nor did he give his men the signal to do so. Instead he called for a whiskey, drank it, and then stood thinking.

'That guy's either loco or dangerous,' he pronounced finally, as Charlie stood beside him.

'Loco,' Charlie decided. 'He must be to wear that get-up he'd gotten on. No man in his right mind would even be found dead in it!'

'Don't be a damned fool,' Bannock said curtly. 'You can't judge a guy by his clothes. He's eddicated for one thing, and that's what I don't like. Seems like a lot of book readin' does things to 'em. All them big words he slings about mean somethin', and he's grinnin' like hell to himself because we don't know what.'

'Look, Jack, as I said before, if he gits to be mayor, it'll be a cinch for us. And if it's Taylor, we know already he'll do as he's told. And if it's you, there's nothin' more to say. Just the same,' Charlie finished, 'I can't see why you didn't just call yourself mayor and have done with it instead of goin' to all this blasted trouble.'

'Because it's safest,' the outlaw answered. 'The folks was pretty nearly ready to start somethin' when I wiped out the sheriff and to have done the same thing to the mayor might have made them tough. Let 'em think they're havin' an election and they'll keep quiet. Fact remains, I'm goin' to lie low in this town no matter who's in power.'

'But why *this* town?' Charlie asked, puzzled. 'Why can't we shove on to some place where the odds ain't so tough?'

'Because I don't choose – now shut up! You talk a durned sight too much!'

Evidently Meredith's words to the easy-going people of Mountain Peak had had more effect than he expected, for by the following evening, after the voting had been progressing all day in the main hall of the town's chapel, there was no longer any doubt but what Meredith had been elected as the mayor, and by a majority of some hundreds – a telling number in such a small community.

Bannock, on the rostrum at the end of the hall with the other two candidates, stood scowling as the results were announced.

'OK, Homburg, so you win,' he growled, suppressing his fury. 'But I'll tell you one thing: I've planned to stay in this town, and that means I ain't leavin' for you or anybody else, see?'

'There are ways of making you go,' Meredith responded. 'The votes of the people satisfy me that they will, in a crisis, stand solidly behind me. That was one reason why I participated in this somewhat Gilbertian election, so as to see if they prefer justice to gun-law.'

'Who's this Gilbert?' the outlaw snapped. 'Some guy you've been keepin' outa sight?'

'Kindly consider the observation as not uttered. I was merely referring to a witty writer of light opera.' Meredith sighed. 'To revert to the matter in hand: you have five satellites all as murderous as yourself. I have the backing of exactly three hundred and eighty-seven people, my number of votes. On their behalf I'm telling you to go, or in time be made to. I'm also telling you that if you shoot anybody in this town without justifiable reason I'll order your execution and, as mayor, be legally entitled to do so.'

'Smart, ain't you?' the outlaw sneered. 'You seem to be forgettin' that you ain't got a sheriff.'

'I have already selected the new sheriff – my son here.'

The outlaw's face darkened as he looked at Bart seated at the back of the rostrum, Jane by his side, together with one or two of

48

the town elders.

'Couldn't ha' made a better choice, Homburg!' a man called from the audience. 'I reckon Bart Meredith is OK by us for sheriff.'

'Yeah, he's a straight shooter, and—'

'Wait a minute!' Bannock interrupted, whipping out his gun and moving it around indecisively. 'I'm nominating my own candidate for that job – Charlie here.'

'That can't be!' Bart snapped.

'I think it can. I've got the gun and I can shoot faster and straighter than any man in here. The only thing these sorta folks can figure out is hardware.'

'Are you sure of that?' Meredith asked calmly, taking his gun leisurely from its holster as the outlaw watched him in suspicion. With unhurried movements he inspected the weapon carefully and then nodded, smiling at Bannock.

'You seem determined to do everything by the rule of the gun, so let us settle the issue once and for all– You observe the hanging oil lamps up there in the roof?'

The outlaw looked towards the centre of the hall where from the rough timber beams there hung two big lamps on a long, tightly spliced length of cord. Sensing what was coming the men and women beneath them moved quickly to one side and left a clear space.

'Our next moves, my friend, will settle for all time which law there is to be in this town – mine as mayor, or yours as gunman.'

'Yeah?'

'Yes. If you can shoot through that cord and drop the lamps to the floor you win, and I'll declare my mayor-ship void and let you run things your own way.'

'Hold on, Dad!' Bart objected. 'Are you crazy? I know you're a pretty good shot, but I'll gamble that Bannock's a better one. It's far too long a chance!'

'Let me finish outlining my scheme, Son... If you fail,' Meredith resumed, his eyes fixed on the outlaw, 'the day will be mine, and having so shamed yourself as a poor marksman you can hardly insist on gun-law, can you? Now, would you like to take the first shot?'

The outlaw looked vaguely puzzled as if he could not quite fathom this sudden test of skill. Then, levelling his gun he took careful aim and fired. There was a murmur from the assembly as the hanging lamps remained untouched.

'What in hell went wrong, Jack?' Charlie

demanded blankly. 'I ain't never known you to miss before!'

'Somethin' phoney about this!' Bannock said harshly. 'I don't see how I could have missed!'

'The fact remains, sir, that you did,' Meredith commented. 'Maybe I can rectify the error...' and he aimed his own gun carefully.

It exploded, jolting his arm back sharply. With a crash the lamps hit the floor, leaving behind a hanging length of cord frayed at the end.

For a second or two, Bannock stared blankly, and in that time Meredith's gun prodded him hard in the ribs.

'Get out, Bannock,' he ordered, his moon-like face expressionless. 'Get out, and don't ever come back! If I ever see you around here again I'll shoot you dead. I warned you earlier about drawing the wrong conclusion from my baby face.'

Bannock looked about him helplessly, still baffled by his bad marksmanship, and also realizing that the temper of the people in the hall was not to be trifled with. His vaunted power as a dead shot had collapsed and with it all chance of instituting the law of the gun – for the time being, anyway.

'See Bannock and his friends on their

way,' Meredith ordered, as the men and women moved forward. 'Drive the lot of them to the end of the street and make sure they do not come back.'

This time there was no hesitation amongst the people and Meredith stood watching with a dry smile as the hapless gunman and his five cohorts were roughly seized and bundled out of the chapel. Bart watched too, Jane by his side, and both of them looked mystified.

'Well, Dad, you certainly held him up to ridicule and got him kicked out. Let's hope he'll stay out,' Bart commented. 'But he's got such a terrific reputation as a gunman I can't imagine how he missed that target, slender though it was. I expected to see those lamps drop the moment he fired.'

'Did you, Son?' There was an inscrutable grin curving Meredith's full lips. 'Ridicule an egoist like that and he takes a nosedive to defeat. That was my intention. I knew he would finally pull a gun on us, that being the only technique he understands.'

'But why didn't he shoot straight?' Jane asked.

'He probably did.' Meredith smiled, lowering his voice. 'But, unfortunately for him, that was of little avail because earlier in the proceedings I took the liberty of removing his gun from its holster, loading it with blanks, and then replacing it. At that time he was so busy watching who was voting for him he failed to notice my – hmm – light-fingered activities.'

'Trust you to think of that,' Bart grinned. 'Anyway, congratulations on your own marksmanship!'

'I have an admission in that regard. During the night – having in mind that this little gunplay strategy might be called for later – I visited this chapel and cut the lamp cord, replacing it with a string connection between the severed ends and afterwards plaiting the cord into place so that the deception, from the floor, could not be seen.'

Bart glanced at Jane and she gave a solemn wink.

'As long as the lamps had no sudden strain upon them they were safe enough – but any jolt would snap the string instantly. So you see, I had merely to fire at the lamps themselves – a target I could not possibly miss – and the impact was sufficient to snap the string.'

'And if the folks find the dent of where your bullet hit the lamps, what then?' Jane asked, a mischievous glint in her eye.

'That can be written off as the bad marksmanship of Mr Bannock. Incidentally, the noise of the bullet striking the lamps was not heard, chiefly because I aimed at the base from which there is no ringing note. You see how beautifully everything fits in?'

'Doesn't miss a point, does he?' Jane asked, smiling at Bart.

'I try not to,' Meredith confessed modestly, then added in a louder voice, 'If you are ready, Son, I think the swearing-in ceremony which will make you sheriff can commence, with these good people here as our witnesses.'

# 3

## EXIT CHARLIE

Five miles outside the town, John Bannock drew rein under the stars and sat waiting for his five comrades to catch up with him. Here they were completely alone, with only the brooding grey of the mountains to their rear, and the chilly breath of the night wind, with its aroma of cedar and pine, disturbing the tranquility.

'We'll be safe enough pitching camp in those mountain foothills,' the outlaw declared. 'But first there's things to talk over.'

He set the example by dropping from his horse, and his men did likewise. They settled finally in the dry ditch nearby, lighted cigarettes, then considered the dim shadow of each others' faces in the starlight.

'Ain't no use denyin' one thing,' Charlie commented sourly. 'I reckon that pot-bellied mayor weren't kiddin' when he said he'd shoot us on sight if we go back.'

'And you were the stupid bonehead who

said it'd be a natch if he got made mayor,' Bannock growled.

'That was mostly your fault! You shouldn't have missed that lamp target. I've never known you to put up such a lousy show.'

'Mind what you're sayin', feller! I fired straight, as I always do.' Bannock frowned over the remembrance of the incident for a moment; then he tugged out his right-hand gun and snapped it open, unloading five cartridges into his palm. He peered at them in the starlight, then, 'The dirty, two-timin' ornery cuss!' he exploded in fury. 'Blanks! No wonder I missed! Some jigger switched my real slugs – pot-belly's work!'

He flung the blanks down in the ditch and began to reload the chambers with genuine bullets from the belt about his waist.

'That fat guy's sure got no flies on him,' Charlie wagged his head. 'Took you for a nice ride, Jack, didn't he?'

'Aw, shut up! I'll git even, don't you sweat. Somethin's gotta be done, and it's gotta be done quick.'

Silence. Then one of the other men said, 'Like Charlie, I don't see why you need stick around a dump like Mountain Peak, Jack – 'specially now that moon-faced mayor's on the prod for us. Surely there's less tough places to lie doggo?'

'There's more to it than that, Sam,' Bannock answered. 'I wasn't goin' to tell you mugs right away why I chose Mountain Peak as a hideout, but I guess things have changed. We'll need to work together from now on.'

'So you've been holdin' out on us?' Charlie asked, surprised. 'What gives?'

'Somewhere around Mountain Peak,' Bannock said, obvious reluctance in his tone, 'there's two hundred thousand dollars in Wells-Fargo gold. There's been a reward out fur the finder of it for about ten years now. I don't want the chicken-feed reward – but I *do* want the gold! Some owlhoot stole it along with other cargo from a Wells-Fargo stage and buried the lot around here, then cashed in his chips. I heard about it when we were back east at Arrowhead.'

'And you didn't say nothin'!' Charlie blazed. 'You're only admittin' it now because you need us to stick around this dangerous territory to help you find the gold! OK, where the hell is it?'

'You think I'd be clownin' around like this if I knew?' the outlaw asked sourly. 'It's probably somewhere in those mountain foothills. But we can't make a base camp there without food and drink and fodder for the cayuses. That's why I tried to take over Mountain Peak. We're not ridin' out on two hundred thousand in gold without good reason – but we can't live without food from the town. Only one thing for it – remove the opposition before it can remove us.'

'And git drilled doin' it!' one of the men commented.

'Not if we're careful. The only two we need worry about in Mountain Peak are Homburg and that dude son of his he's made into a sheriff. But this time we'll take care of 'em the tough way. No election, no nothin'. Do as they're told or git shot.'

'I reckon we should have done it that way at first,' one of the men growled. 'That guy Homburg ain't nobody's fool. It'll be tough to git near enough to plug him, Jack. He'll either see you first or have somebody watchin' who will.'

'There's an easier way than that,' Bannock replied, musing. 'It's a job for you, Charlie, while the rest of us keep out in readiness to attack. Now listen – here's the set-up…'

Of necessity Bart's appointment as sheriff demanded that much of his time be spent in the town away from the ranch. His father also, to fulfil his mayoral duties, had to be in the town to prepare his various far-reaching plans for the betterment of its sleepy denizens.

It meant that the Slanting-F had to be deserted for long periods, and Jane left alone. Although she could shoot as fast and straight as any man, Bart was definitely uneasy. So he did the only thing possible and engaged three men, upon whom he knew he could rely, to take care of the ranch activities and have an eye to the girl's safety at the same time. More than this he felt he could not do.

All these moves were being secretly observed. There was hardly a moment when either Bannock or Charlie was not surreptitiously watching the Slanting-F and the comings and goings of its inhabitants. They were waiting for the chance that they knew must come sooner or later.

Altogether a week passed whilst these new arrangements were made, then, at twilight one evening, Charlie went into action. He had seen both Bart and his father depart for the town an hour before and Jane herself was alone in the ranch house. In the corrals, settling the steers for the night, were the three men who were running the cattle side

59

of the ranch.

Charlie rode straight in from the surrounding pastureland, crossed the wide yard, then dismounted. As he had judged, the men in the corrals failed to observe his arrival in the dim, fast deepening twilight.

He took his horse round the side of the ranch house, out of their sight, tethered it under the window of what he judged to be the living-room, and then returned to the front porch. His knocking brought Jane to the door. She stood back with a little start as she recognized him.

'Surprised, huh?' he asked briefly, casting a lascivious eye over her slim figure in its white silk blouse and black riding pants. He kicked the door shut behind him and then dropped the bar back into place. 'Git into that livin'-room, sweetheart – quick!'

For answer Jane dived her hand into her blouse, reaching for a shoulder-holster, but a heavy shove sent her stumbling into the living-room and she collapsed in a wicker chair. Her gun was snatched from its hiding place and she found herself staring at the .38 in Charlie's hand.

'Try shoutin' for help and I'll plug you,' he warned grimly. 'Now git yourself a sheet of paper and somethin' to write with. I'll tell what to write.'

Jane looked at him fixedly for a moment, then out through the nearest window towards the dimness of the corrals.

'You won't get any help from those three guys out there. They don't even know I'm here – and if they come snoopin' I'll take care of 'em. Now git that paper and pen and make it quick!'

Jane reflected for a moment then rose and went across to the bureau, settling down in front of it. Charlie followed her, remaining a foot away with his gun handy. She found a pen and ink and looked up at him in troubled silence.

'OK, sister – start writin' – "I've been taken to Rocky Canyon by one of Bannock's men–" And put a dash after it, like you'd been interrupted.'

'What's the meaning of this?' Jane demanded.

'Never you mind – just git them words written!'

The girl hesitated, then the gun prodded hard in the small of her back. She wrote the words down, added a dash, and waited nervously, replacing the lid of the ink bottle. Charlie picked up the note and studied it, nodded, then screwed it up in his palm.

Finally he tossed it on the floor near the rug where it could not help but be noticed by anybody coming in.

'Now you're goin' places, sweetheart. Start movin' to that window on the left there. My hoss is just outside.'

'I'm not going anywhere!' Jane broke out in fury. 'Just what are you planning to do with me?'

'That's up to Jack Bannock. All I know is that that precious husband of yours, and his pot-bellied pop, will find that note when they come back – and then they'll come lookin' for you. When they do they'll run smack into an ambuscade and be taken care of.' He grinned wolfishly. 'You're a decoy, sister, and if you make one wrong move it'll be curtains–'

Jane swung, diving for the nearest window. She made a vain effort to wrench it up and scream for help, then Charlie's powerful arms were about her, smothering her screams and forcing her towards the further window outside which stood his horse.

Strong as she was Jane had not the power to defeat the iron-muscled outlaw. She found herself pushed through the window-frame, her kerchief now tied across her mouth to prevent her shouting; then she dropped heavily into the saddle. Charlie landed immediately behind her, his gun in her back once more. One savage jab of his spurs was sufficient to set the horse bounding across the yard and through the open gateway.

For a moment the three men just about to leave the corrals saw what was happening and shouted hoarsely – then the short twilight faded with characteristic abruptness and Charlie and the girl were lost to sight.

An hour later when Bart and Meredith returned to the spread – accompanied by the acting ranch foreman, who had ridden into town to fetch them – they found the other two men waiting, grim-faced, with the note the girl had written lying smoothed out on the table.

Bart strode across and picked up the note, his father looking over his shoulder as he read it in the light of the oil lamp.

'OK, that settles it,' Bart snapped, crushing the note in his hand. 'We've got to get after her right away, Dad. It's a plain case of snatching!'

'Looks like it, Son.'

'Have you boys tried to do anything yet?' Bart demanded of the other men.

The two men who had been left behind

shook their heads. One of them replied, 'It seemed more like a matter for you to give orders, than for us to go dashing off on our own account.'

'Hell and damnation! Your delaying things like this may have got my wife into God knows what danger!' Bart raved at them. 'If you had any damned sense you'd have—'

'Done exactly what they have done, sir – nothing,' Meredith commented, laying the note aside after studying it again.

The men looked relieved but Bart frowned.

'Jane's been abducted and you stand there saying that we should do nothing about it! Well, I'm going to – and if you're scared of helping me you can do the other thing! I'm not standing around here while—'

'Naturally Jane must be rescued,' Meredith intervened calmly, 'but do you suppose for one moment that a gunman would ever have given her time to write a note like this, even to the extent of permitting her to remove notepaper from the bureau and unscrew the top of an ink bottle – and then reseal it? Hardly, Son, hardly!'

'Which adds up to what?' Bart asked impatiently. 'Stop talking in confounded riddles, Dad!'

'This note is a decoy, Son, I'm convinced

of it!' Meredith said, raising it from the table.

'You mean – to get us into a trap?'

'Exactly, Son! And that being so, I'll have to make certain preparations.' Meredith tossed down the note, then added, 'They may take me about ten minutes...'

'Every minute's valuable but I suppose you know what you're doing,' Bart said. 'OK, you hop to it. I'll be making sure we've plenty of ammunition.'

Meredith nodded and departed into an adjoining bedroom. Bart looked across at the three men who were still waiting for instructions.

'Dad and I will handle this ourselves,' he decided. 'You had better guard the premises in case anything else happens.'

The men nodded and went out. Bart turned to an inspection of his .45s and made sure that he had a fully loaded cartridge belt, then after a while he glanced up as his father returned.

Over his shoulders Meredith was carrying two roughly made dummies of sackcloth and straw. The larger one was dressed in an old suit of his clothes, and over the other shoulder was a dummy dressed as Bart, both of them supplied with old hats.

'Now what?' Bart asked blankly. 'This is no time for playing games, Dad!'

'Hardly a game, Son, I assure you. This will be a case of the decoyers decoyed.'

'I still don't get it.'

'Right now you don't need to. We'll put my little strategy into effect when we have almost reached Rocky Canyon: then you'll soon see for yourself what I have devised.'

Without asking any further questions, Bart led the way quickly out of the living-room and to the horses. Meredith slung the dummies over his stallion and then mounted heavily to the saddle, fixing his Homburg firmly in position. This done, he set the massive animal galloping ponderously after Bart's much swifter mare.

Presently both men drew level but said no word, riding steadily under the stars and dawning moonrise. As near as they could judge, the mountains – where lay Rocky Canyon – were some three miles distant.

It was when they finally began to near the bend in the trail that led to the canyon that Meredith called a halt.

Bart slid down from the saddle, watching in some surprise and then interest as Meredith affixed the dummies to the two horses, his own effigy on the stallion and Bart's on the mare. When finally they were held in an upright position by cords, Meredith slapped the withers of each animal in turn and sent them cantering forward.

'I'm hoping, Son, that we may draw the fire of our unpleasant friends,' he explained. 'In this dim starlight the dummies should pass for us. Our two horses should bolt and run on at the noise of the gunfire and, because they are travelling light, should give the outlaws quite a run for their money. Whilst they are chasing them we can start searching for Jane. She should be nearby somewhere.'

Meredith had barely finished speaking before there was a sudden rattling of shots from the trail not half a mile away. Instantly, he and Bart hurried forward, keeping well to the side of the trail. This brought them to a position where they were able to see beyond the bend.

They were met with the sight of the gun-men, firing savagely, hurtling their horses into the night in the wake of what seemed to be two dimly visible riders. Within a few seconds the thunder of their pursuing hoofs had died away.

'You did it, Dad,' Bart murmured. 'A nice piece of strategy!'

'Thank you, Son. We've gained a breathing space to look for Jane. Let's use it!'

They continued along the edge of the trail, looking keenly about them but failing to notice anything but mesquite bushes, long grass, and the dusty twisted whiteness that marked the trail. Then after a while Meredith gripped his son's arm and pointed.

Bart gazed steadily and then became aware of a dark silhouette cut against the starry backdrop. A man stood perhaps a dozen yards away on a rising piece of ground, obviously alert for the first sign of trouble.

'Definitely a look-out,' Bart whispered. 'Luckily he isn't turned in our direction at the moment.'

'Since this whole business was an ambuscade, this point is probably not the outlaws' normal hide-out,' Meredith murmured. 'If you will allow me, Son, I'll take out that sentry.'

'Go to it,' Bart agreed. 'I'll start and look for Jane whilst you do your stuff.'

Meredith nodded and, Bart a little way behind him, began to creep forward. It was amazing how a man of his huge dimensions could be so silent. He travelled on hands and knees, making no noise in the soft sand – until at length he was within two yards of the motionless gunman as he stood glancing about him, entirely unaware as yet of danger.

Meredith stood upright, measured his distance, and sprang.

The gunman heard the sound at the last second but it was too late for him to do anything about it. Eighteen stone of flesh collided with him violently, stomach first, and knocked him backwards. Though he was on his feet again almost at once, the human battering ram came again and sent him spinning. His gun was wrenched from his hand and he looked up dazedly at the fat giant in the absurd Homburg outlined against the stars.

'Get on your feet!' Meredith snapped.

The man rose slowly. 'Homburg!' he breathed. 'I'll be damned!' His voice identified him to Meredith – and Bart as he came forward – as Charlie, Bannock's right-hand man.

'You'll be damned all right, if you don't tell me where my wife is,' Bart said venomously. 'Talk, or I'll beat it out of you.'

'With Fatty's gun coverin' me that shouldn't be difficult,' Charlie sneered.

'Leather your gun, Dad,' Bart said, glancing at him. 'Time I taught this gunnie a few tricks.'

As Meredith slipped the .45 in its holster, Charlie lashed out almost immediately at Bart with his right, missed, and instead received a left that struck him violently under the jaw. He sat down in the sand, got up and lunged – but to his surprise Bart was not there.

Then it seemed that two hands came from nowhere and seized him, one on the wrist and the other on the back of the neck. Before he could comprehend what had happened he had been thrown through the air, and crashed on his face amidst sharp-bladed scrub-grass. Then Bart was astride him, his fingers gripping the man's ankle and twisting it gently, but with excruciating torment.

'Splendid, Son,' Meredith approved. 'The old judo grip, I observe. Decidedly a telling weapon in this land of lawless men.'

'Git off'n me,' Charlie panted. 'You're breakin' my blasted leg!'

'You never said anything truer,' Bart retorted. 'I mean to go right on breaking it unless you tell me where my wife is and take me to her.' He turned the ankle a shade further and the puncher gasped and struggled futilely in the judo hold. He felt perspiration start out on his face and excruciating pain went the length of his leg. But still he refused to talk.

Knowing that Bannock and his men might return at any moment, Bart did not hesitate any further. He gave a wrench that brought a scream from the man and then a chattering chaos of words...

'OK, *OK!* I'll take you to her. She's up in the hills. For God's sake let go of my ankle!'

'All right, so she's up in the hills,' Bart said, getting up and aiming his gun. 'We'll go there right now – and if you're fooling, Charlie, it'll be for the last time. Go on – get walking!'

The gunman obeyed, limping heavily. Meredith had found his horse and taken charge of it, foiling any sudden escape attempt by the outlaw.

Altogether it took the trio nearly thirty minutes to reach the mountain foothills, and they began to follow a rough acclivity, which brought them finally to a point some 500 feet from ground level. Here, on a narrow rimrock, a cave presently became visible in the bright moonlight, and outside it the gunman came to a stop.

'In there,' he directed sullenly.

Bart wandered into the cave cautiously, Meredith remaining on the alert outside and holding the outlaw's horse. Within seconds

Bart had found the girl and released her.

'What happened, Jane?' he asked quickly, his arm about her. 'You hurt or anything?'

'No, I'm all right. Only I've been scared witless as to what might happen next. How did you manage to find me so easily?'

'It wasn't easy – far from it. Dad and I had to make one of Bannock's gunmen talk.' Keeping his arm about her Bart led her out of the cave; then he looked at the gunman and snapped, 'Luckily for you, you spoke the truth. Now I've got my wife back safely, nothing else matters. But if you show yourself anywhere near my ranch or the town again I'll shoot you down without the option. Remember that! Come on, Dad. Let's get out of here.'

'First, Son, I have a little matter to deal with.' Meredith sounded thoughtful as he looked about him.

'What matter?' Bart asked impatiently. 'Bannock and his boys are liable to come this way at any moment.'

'We'll deal with them if they do,' Meredith responded calmly. 'But first I've something to ask our unspeakable friend.' He turned and faced the gunman squarely.

'I need you to tell me what *other* reason you men have for staying in this district. It isn't just so you can lie low. So – what is your real reason?'

'Who told you we were lyin' low?' Charlie stood with his back to the canyon, hands slightly raised, his face dimly white in the gloom.

Meredith smiled. 'Since I became mayor, and my son here sheriff, we have learned many things – including the fact that all of you men are wanted by the authorities. From my point of view it seems odd that you remain so determined to make Mountain Peak your hide-out when you could choose many other quieter towns.'

'We're stickin' around because the boss don't mean to be bested by you and this dude son of yours,' Charlie retorted, still defiant.

'Not a very satisfactory answer, I'm afraid,' Meredith said, advancing a few more steps, gun in one hand and the reins of the gunman's mare in the other. The few steps brought him so close to Charlie that he was at the very edge of the rimrock and could go back no further. He came to a stop and gave a startled look below and behind him.

'You have brought this on yourself,' Meredith said implacably. 'My stomach is now approximately eight inches from yours. I have only to suddenly jut mine forward in order to knock you clean off this ledge into that somewhat murky-looking ravine below...'

'You wouldn't!' the outlaw panted. 'I don't rate bein' bumped off like that!'

'You murder at random and yet don't think you should be wiped out in return! You'd better think again! If you want to go on living tell me why you and the other men insist on remaining in this district!'

Charlie edged uneasily until he felt the stones at the edge of the trail sliding under his weight. Relentlessly Meredith moved forward a few more inches. Charlie began to breathe even harder.

*'It's – it's for gold!'* he blurted out suddenly.

'Gold!' Meredith echoed, surprised. 'Explain yourself!'

'There's two hundred thousand dollars' worth of gold around here somewhere – part of a Wells-Fargo robbery ten years ago. There's still a reward bein' offered for it. Jack Bannock heard of it and he aims to stick around the territory 'til he finds it.'

'So that's it?' Meredith mused. 'Thank you, my friend. I knew there had to be a definite reason for such love of this district.'

He withdrew slightly and released hold of the mare's reins. With his fingers he suddenly tickled the creature's belly – and the result was instantaneous. The mare shied and lashed out one of her back legs. Charlie, standing right behind the animal, received a steel-shod hoof clean in the face and with a howl of pain and terror he reeled backwards into space and sailed down into the gloom of the canyon.

Bart felt Jane convulse a little against him.

'Extraordinary,' Meredith commented, looking about him in wide-eyed innocence. 'I wonder why the mare kicked like that?'

'You know why, Randle,' Jane said, turning to look at him. 'I saw what you did to the mare.'

Meredith moved to the canyon's edge, peered into it, and raised his Homburg in mock reverence. Then he turned back to where Bart and the girl were standing.

'That's one less outlaw we have to worry about,' Bart said. 'Now let's get out of here before the others get back – I can't understand what's delaying them.'

'Let's not concern ourselves about that,' Meredith said. 'Our main object is to get back to the ranch and then decide what we must do next to deal with these gold hunters. Jane can ride this mare, Son, and you and I will walk. Perhaps, our own horses will return home in time, unless in his fury at discovering the dummies Bannock has destroyed the animals.'

Bart helped Jane to the mare's saddle and presently the return journey down the narrow mountain trail commenced. Every moment all three of them expected the outlaw or one of his men to appear – but nothing transpired.

Even though they took every short cut they knew it was nearly two hours later and in the small hours of the morning before the bulk of the Slanting-F became visible beyond a rise of the land. At the sight of the oil light gleaming from the windows of the living-room Bart gave a frown.

'I told the boys to stop on guard. They surely would not have the blasted nerve to–'

'Something unexpected must have happened,' Meredith interrupted, confident of the integrity of the men concerned. 'I hardly think it can be Bannock, either. Even he wouldn't be fool enough to light the lamps and so give away his presence.'

Bart urged the mare onwards more rapidly, running beside it, Meredith coming up in the rear with his Homburg pushed on to the back of his head and his breathing laboured. Within a few minutes they had reached the yard of the ranch and from here it was only a matter of seconds to gain the living-room.

They burst in upon a surprising sight. Lying upon the long couch under the window was Jacob Taylor, the former mayor, his plump body bloodstained across the chest, his breathing shallow. Beside him were the three men who formed the Slanting-F's outfit. They got up immediately as the trio entered.

'What the devil's been going on here?' Bart asked quickly.

'We were on guard, Mr Meredith, like you told us,' the acting foreman explained, 'when this guy came ridin' in out of the night, pretty well shot to bits. We've done what we can for him but I guess he hasn't got long. He got four slugs in him and one's mighty near the heart.'

'Dad, see that Jane has a drink and a rest,' Bart instructed then he went down on one knee beside the harshly breathing ex-mayor. 'Were you trying to see me, Mr Taylor?' he asked, and at the sound of the voice the man opened his dark eyes.

'Yeah,' he whispered. 'I … was…'

'Why?' Bart urged, shaking the man gently to prevent him relapsing into a coma from which he might not awaken.

The ex-mayor stirred again and coughed thickly. His halting voice continued, 'I wanted ... to tell you Bannock's taken over the town again while you've been away...' He broke off into another cough. 'He says he'll ... shoot you both on sight ... and ... anybody else who sides with – with you...'

Taylor struggled hard for breath and Bart raised his head and shoulders a little.

'I was there when ... he and his men came into the saloon just on closin' time ... I – I was there, remember, when your foreman came to fetch you? I thought to warn you what Bannock means doin' – I guess he thought I was tryin' to leave town to get the authorities and he shot me as I rode out. Somehow ... I ... finished my journey to here and then I – I...'

Taylor became silent, motionless, his gaze fixed on the ceiling. Bart pressed down the eyelids gently and then stood up. He met the worried glance of Jane, then the calm scrutiny of his father.

'A declaration of war,' Meredith commented. 'Bannock must have found out about the dummies on horseback and realized how he had been fooled. He also must have realized that you and I would be busy trying to find Jane – so with us out of the way, he went into town and took it over at the gun-point with his men, which accounts for their non-arrival back at the mountain base.'

'He's not getting away with it,' Bart snapped. 'You and I are mayor and sheriff, Dad, and it's up to us to free the town.'

'I agree with you, Son, but if we make a sudden blind rush into town we'll be walking into trouble and certain death. This requires thinking about. I am a great believer in considered thought before taking action.'

Bart shrugged. 'You seem to be able to size up these scum far better than I.'

'I know human nature, Son. Bannock is a colossal egotist, and as such cannot tolerate ridicule. So the obvious course is for me to think up ways and means of belittling him. There can be no better way to make him writhe.'

'OK. But what about poor Taylor's body? We can't just leave it lying here.'

'I suggest that we have it buried, perform the simple last rites, and have the spot marked with a cross. That is the somewhat primitive way in which corpses are disposed of in this remote spot. As mayor and sheriff we have the authority to do that.'

'And the authority to arrest Bannock for

this night's work and hang him!' Jane declared. 'He shot Mr Taylor! For the life of me I can't see why we need to go through all this monkey business. Why can't you arrest him?'

'There are difficulties, Jane,' Meredith pointed out, still thinking. 'Since Mr Taylor is dead where is our proof of what he said? We might remove the bullets from his body and endeavour to compare them with one from Bannock's revolver – which in the eyes of the authorities in Wilson or Caradoc City would be considered sound evidence – but do you suppose Bannock would give us that chance? No! So for the moment his crime will have to go unpunished, but in the end he will pay for everything in full.'

Bart glanced at the three 'punchers who were still standing beside the door.

'Better get this body out of the way,' he told them. 'Bury it under the sycamore on Mesa Rise. He had no wife, so I guess there's nobody needs telling about what's happened to him. The town lawyer will have to figure out what happens to his property when I give him the facts tomorrow.'

The three men picked up the body between them, carrying it from the room. For a moment or two there was silence, Meredith rubbing his chins and gazing absently at the oil lamp. Finally he seemed to make up his mind and looked at Bart.

'I have a little scheme, Son, once again using the weapon of ridicule, which should have the desired effect.'

'Sounds promising,' Bart said. 'Let's have it.'

'I would prefer to outline the scheme tomorrow and explain then how Jane and yourself fit into it. I also think it would be better if we did not visit the town tomorrow during daylight – that's the very move Bannock is waiting for.'

'But we are sheriff and mayor!' Bart protested. 'If we don't show up in our offices the folks will think we're scared and are leaving Bannock in charge.'

Meredith smiled. 'Any such illusion on that point will be dispelled by what I trust will happen tomorrow evening. I suggest that you get the facts concerning Mr Taylor's death written out, and tomorrow whilst in town – after sunset of course – I will deliver it at the appropriate office. Right now it's not far from dawn, I think we cannot do better than try and get some sleep.'

# 4

## MEREDITH POURS A DRINK

At nightfall the following evening the few citizens in the main street of Mountain Peak were treated to the extraordinary vision of Randle Meredith riding with all the dignity of a caliph into their midst.

His huge grey stallion – which had returned of its own accord to the Slanting-F during the night, Bart's mare arriving some time afterwards – stirred a gentle cloud of dust behind it. Meredith had made one call at the closed lawyer's office down the street and now sat expressionless, his Homburg firmly planted on his head, his right hand resting lightly on his .45. He glanced about him warily but there seemed to be no signs of potential attack as he plodded the horse to the Painted Lady and there dismounted, wheezing with effort.

Three 'punchers lounging against the boardwalk rail regarded him fixedly.

'You loco, Homburg?' one of them enquired. 'Don't you know that Bannock's taken over and is on the prod for you?'

'Since a man can only die once,' Meredith responded, tying the stallion's reins to the hitch rail, 'I am prepared to take a risk. I am something of a fatalist. Kismet, my friends – kismet!'

The 'punchers stared blankly at him, then at each other.

Meredith went up the boardwalk steps majestically, the wood creaking under his weight. His great equator burst apart the two batwings as he strode into the Painted Lady and stood looking about him in the tobacco-fumed atmosphere. The moment he appeared, the buzz of conversation and activity slowed, then stopped. Every eye became fixed on him – frightened eyes, wondering eyes, cynical eyes.

His gaze moved towards the bar-counter where John Bannock was standing, a hard grin on his now cleanly shaven, bronzed face.

'Come right in, Homburg,' he invited drily. 'My lookout tipped me off you was on your way. Like a drink? Not often I git the chance to stand a town's mayor some liquor.'

With the grace of a baby elephant Meredith rolled across towards the bar and then beamed on the outlaw disarmingly.

'Thank you for your phoney hospitality. However, I am not addicted to liquor – but a lemonade would be welcome, just to remove the dust of the trail.'

'*What* did you say?' Bannock asked blankly.

'A lemonade. The barkeep understands my requirements exactly,' Meredith explained, glancing at him.

'Sure, Mr Meredith,' the man assented, and pushed across a glass and an opened bottle of mineral. 'Keep 'em specially for you.'

With perfect urbanity Meredith poured himself a drink, then as he drained it from the glass his round blue eyes considered the grim-faced outlaw.

'If I live to be ninety I'll never figure you,' Bannock muttered.

'The chances of that are somewhat remote,' Meredith replied pleasantly, putting his glass down. 'I assume you permitted me to enter this town without being shot for some very good reason of your own? One that is directed towards my ultimate detriment?'

'Yeah. Why should I have a man risk takin' a distance shot at you – and maybe gettin' plugged back – when I can just plug you point blank, right where you stand now?'

'Why indeed?' Meredith shrugged. 'Granting, of course, that I permit such a thing.'

'Cut the jabber, Homburg! Why you come here at all with me and my boys runnin' the place I don't know. I didn't think kindly of them dummies you fixed last night. We chased 'em for miles afore we found out the trick!'

'I have to thank you for not shooting our horses. They both found their way back home to the ranch.'

'I would have done, but they was too quick gettin' away. That was your last trick, Homburg. I aim to git both you an' the dude who calls himself sheriff, and who's too leery to show his mug around here.'

'Your threats are becoming somewhat monotonous,' Meredith sighed. 'It's time you knew exactly where I stand. I am still the legal mayor of this town and I intend to use my power. I came in here for one reason only: to accuse you of the murder of Jacob Taylor last night.'

The men nearest Bannock became suddenly more attentive, their hands resting on their guns.

'I didn't murder the jigger,' the outlaw snapped, 'even though he deserved it.'

'I know that it was at your behest that he

was shot. Because I have no definite evidence I cannot have you hanged, as you should be – but I have other ways of exacting justice. Last night your friend Charlie – your right-hand man I believe – met his death.'

'Yeah?' Bannock's eyes slitted. 'I was wonderin' where he'd gotten to...'

'You'll find his body in the foothills. It makes the score even, Bannock. You killed Taylor, and lost Charlie–'

'You mean you killed him, huh? Probably shot him in the back!'

'He met with an accident. A frisky mare saw fit to lash out her hoof at the very moment the unspeakable Charlie was standing on the edge of a chasm. I'm afraid he took a nose-dive into the depths.'

'You expect me to believe a blasted story like that?'

'That's your problem,' Meredith continued calmly. 'I am warning you here and now that if you kill anybody else you will also lose others. In the end, Bannock, if you persist in eliminating people who get in your way there'll only be one person left upon whom justice can be taken – yourself. A man for a man every time. Understand?'

'You can forget your loco scheme,' Bannock sneered. 'I'll wipe out who I like and when I like, and you won't be around to do anythin' about it!'

The outlaw's right-hand gun flashed up into his fingers and remained pointed. 'This time it ain't loaded with blanks,' he said bitterly. 'Better say your prayers, Homburg!'

Meredith poured out some more lemonade, drawing back his right foot a little as it rested on the rail at the base of the counter.

'Something you should know first, Bannock. I know why you are so anxious to stay in this territory. Charlie was good enough to inform me before he died that you are searching for two hundred thousand dollars in Wells-Fargo gold!'

Instantly the people in the saloon began talking excitedly, and Meredith beamed as he looked around on them.

'*You damned fool!*' Bannock grated furiously. 'That's about bust wide open my chances of lookin' for the gold in peace! Now every durned jigger in the territory will be searchin' too!'

Meredith smiled. 'I hope it starts a stampede.' He finished his drink and put the empty glass back on the counter then with vicious suddenness he slammed out his right foot, toe first. It cracked on the outlaw's shin and he jolted and yelped at the same time, hopping on one foot. Meredith took two swift strides forward and butted out his huge stomach. Overbalanced on his one leg the outlaw crashed down in the sawdust. He got to his knees and then glared round at his men.

'Why the blue hell didn't you shoot him?' he yelled.

'Couldn't risk it, Jack, with you in the way,' one of the men objected. 'We might have hit you as well.'

'Quite so,' Meredith agreed genially, his own guns clamped in each hand. 'Few men are willing to risk shooting their leader, or so I understand from the somewhat lurid dime novels I have read. Kindly throw your hardware on the floor, gentlemen, and you, Bannock, can stand up. Unless you like impersonating a dog?'

There was a clatter as the guns were thrown on the floor and, because he could do nothing else, Bannock rose slowly. He stood glaring and shaking his savagely kicked leg.

'Now there's a score to settle.' Meredith explained. 'I have taken the liberty of having my son and his wife come over here, and at the moment they are waiting for me to finish these preliminaries.' Raising his voice he called, 'Whenever you are ready, Son! Madam! The coast is entirely clear.'

Frowning, Bannock and his men watched Jane and then Bart come through the bat-wings towards the bar-counter, followed by the stares of the men and women at the tables.

'Nice work, Dad,' Bart said. 'You handled it all right, though I'd much rather have been in it on myself.'

'What sort of a farce do you call this?' Bannock demanded.

'It's no farce, Bannock. Last night you caused this young woman a good deal of anxiety, not to say physical shock, with your abduction. I have decided that you shall apologize to her, here and now.'

'*Apologize?*' Bannock suddenly burst into a yell of laughter. Resting his elbows back against the counter he shook with merriment, his eyes closed and his mouth open.

Quickly Meredith reached out and took a lighted cigar from the man nearest him. With a neat movement he tapped a full inch of grey ash into the outlaw's gaping jaws.

With a spluttering gasp Bannock ceased laughing and wiped his mouth savagely with the back of his hand. 'Blast you to hell!' he roared. 'I'll–'

90

'I object to laughter when I have made a serious statement,' Meredith handed the cigar back to its amazed owner as he sat at the nearby table. Apologize – *now!*'

'Go to hell!'

Meredith toyed with his right-hand gun for a moment as he reflected; then he dropped it to the floor, apparently by accident. He stooped, but instead of picking up the weapon he gripped the outlaw's nearer ankle and heaved, flinging him over helplessly. This time he had no chance to get up for eighteen stone planted itself with crushing weight on his midriff.

'There are times,' Meredith commented, 'when I wonder what is so tough about you men of the West. Perfectly simple methods defeat you every time. Now, sir, your apology if you please!'

Bannock writhed and struggled desperately but he could not budge his massive assailant. Since no apology was forthcoming Meredith reached up with one hand to a brandy bottle on the counter, uncorked it, then seized the gunman's nose and forced it back. He was compelled to open his mouth wide and the brand flooded into it like water down a sluice.

'This drink is on me, Bannock. I am prepared to pay for gallons of brandy just as long as I achieve the desired effect.'

'*Gug...*' Bannock responded, wriggling and sucking breath into his scorched throat.

Meredith tipped the bottle up again. This time he completely emptied it and Bannock, slopped with the spirit and nearly purple from lack of wind and the fire devouring him to his vitals, could hardly speak.

'Another bottle?' Meredith suggested, reaching up to the counter and plonking down money to cover the bottle he had already used.

'*No, no, wait!*' Bannock choked. 'For – for God's sake! I'll apologize! Can't you see when you're damned near killin' me?'

Meredith put the uncorked bottle back on the counter and stood up, his gun ready. Bart took a step to one side, his own gun still levelled. Half intoxicated, the outlaw reeled on to his feet and stared blearily at Jane.

'I'm – sorry,' he gulped. 'I reckon I – didn't oughta have snatched you.'

'Try it again anywhere within range of my guns and I'll shoot you down,' Bart snapped. 'Meantime, I've my own payment to make for last night's work–' He broke off as he brought up his fist in a lightning uppercut.

Dazed as he was, Bannock was unable to dodge the blow. He spun round on his heels and dropped motionless, face down in the sawdust. Meredith considered him, then turned him over with his boot.

'Horizontal again,' he beamed. 'Our friend has an extraordinary penchant for impersonating dogs. Maybe because he *is* one!' His baby-blue eyes shifted to the four remaining gunmen by the counter.

'You can learn from this object lesson. I would be disinclined to be loyal to a man who can be so easily beaten as our canine friend on the floor here. He hardly looks like a tough leader at the moment, does he? Sodden with brandy and sawdust all over his face and hair. Now, just one final thing...'

Meredith picked up Bannock's gun. Wedging the barrel between the bar and the footrail he forced his great weight down on the butt, resulting in the revolver finishing up in the shape of a letter 'L'.

'Give this to him when he recovers, with my compliments,' Meredith said, tossing the ruined weapon on the counter, where the four 'punchers looked at it dazedly. 'I'm advising you to get out of town. Remember – a life for a life every time from now on.'

With that, leaving the four gunmen and the saloon habitués staring after him. Meredith began to back to the batwings, Bart and Jane on either side of him. They made their retreat swiftly, mounted their horses, and were heading into the night in a matter of seconds. Only when they were halfway back to the Slanting-F did Bart make a comment.

'Frankly, Dad, I don't see what you accomplished tonight, beyond giving Bannock a beating and extracting an insincere apology from him. You also set him up to ridicule, but he's still there to fight again. Why the clowning around? I don't see why we can't get the authorities down here and straighten things out properly.'

Meredith shook his head. 'For all we know Bannock could have men posted to watch the direct trails leading into Caradoc and Wilson City where the authorities are located – and the result would be bullets in our backs. Further, it is technically the job of a mayor and sheriff in a town like this to handle their own troubles, and that I believe is what we should do.'

'But these men are wanted in several States and there's a reward for their apprehension, dead or alive. We could get that and peace and quiet at the same time, if we got the authorities down here to look into things.'

'You are prosperous enough, Son, not to need the reward, and I am sure you are enjoying the struggle to defeat these desperadoes without having to ask the authorities for help. Eventually they will be taken care of, never fear – and handed over, or else killed.'

'You're not fooling me with your explanations, Randle,' Jane remarked drily. 'You're simply enjoying yourself thoroughly, and don't want outside interference! Why not come into the open and admit it?'

Meredith sighed. 'I am afraid, madam, that you have guessed my secret. I have never had such fun since I was a nipper! And I have a plan, which I think will take care of these gentlemen very nicely.'

'All right, maybe there is a risk in trying to get to the authorities,' Bart said. 'The pity is that the railroad isn't operating again yet, after the owners in Wilson City were arrested for what they tried to do here recently.' Bart shrugged. 'Since *we* were responsible for that, I guess we can't complain... OK, I'll go along with you,' Bart finished. 'What's the plan?'

'It is somewhat involved. I'll explain it at

the ranch. Meantime, the best way for us to avoid danger at the moment is to cease going into town as mayor and sheriff. There is no doubt that the next time Bannock sets eyes on us he'll shoot us down – with a new gun, of course.'

'You can't mean that we sit around the ranch and let him retain complete control of Mountain Peak?'

'For the moment – yes. That is part of my strategy. Bannock will probably strike at the ranch if anywhere, so for that we must be prepared. But we will be by no means idle, as you will see when I have outlined my plan.'

Fresh night air and a ducking in the horse-trough in the main street proved sufficient to revive the brandy-stupefied Bannock. His four cohorts, at an end of heaving him in and out of the water, gazed at his dripping figure propped against the trough.

With an effort he stayed on his feet, shivering in the cold wetness of his shirt as the stiff night breeze blew from the mountains.

'What happened to the dude and pot-belly?' he asked sourly. 'They get away?'

'Yeah they sure did,' one of the men, known as Hank, acknowledged. 'They just vamoosed, and from what they said they mean to cause plenty more trouble for us. Homburg told me to give you this, by the way.'

The outlaw took the L-shaped .45 that Hank handed to him. He stared at it fixedly, his face contorted; then with terrific violence he flung it down in the dirt. Reaching out, he snatched a gun from the holster of the man nearest him.

'Smart sort of snake, ain't he?' he breathed. 'I'll blast him for this – just let me set eyes on him again, and–'

'Just a chance you mightn't do anythin' at all,' one of the men growled. 'Homburg must be confident he can beat us because he makes no effort to fetch in a marshal and nail us that way.'

'He's scared,' Bannock sneered.

'No he ain't, Jack. He ain't scared one bit. I reckon he's just playin' around with us. If he'd come into the open and fight with guns we could tackle him, but he don't. He uses all kinds of sneakin' little tricks you just can't weigh up.'

'I tell you he's scared!' Bannock roared. 'Ain't no other explanation – unless he's just plain crazy. Hell, I wish he'd make one break for Wilson City or Caradoc – and that'd finish him. Don't forgit we've got three boys on the watch in turns on both of those trails.'

'If you can trust 'em,' Hank commented doubtfully. 'We recruited 'em from the town community, remember, when they offered to join us. We took a chance on that and so far it's come off, but if they ain't loyal–'

'They are!' Bannock interrupted flatly. 'I know the guys I can trust and they're on the level. Use your brains, damn you! If they wasn't they'd have gotten the authorities from Wilson or Caradoc themselves by now, wouldn't they?'

'Mebbe.'

'Mebbe be damned! Anyways, I guess Homburg is too smart to take a risk like that. He'll try some sneakin' way of gettin' at us...'

Bannock furrowed his brow then at length gave a snort of annoyance.

'The hell with that critter for now. The best thing we can do is start searchin' in earnest for that Wells-Fargo gold and then quit this territory the minute we find it. I don't aim to git myself mixed up with Homburg more'n I can help. I don't believe his story about Charlie's death bein' an accident, and reckon he's a killer at heart.'

'It ain't goin' to be easy to try and find that gold either,' Hank put in morosely. 'Now that everybody knows about it, they'll all be crawlin' like flies round the landscape and gettin' in our way.'

'We can take care of that by warnin' 'em that if they start on a search we'll blast the daylights outa them,' Bannock responded. 'They're a mighty docile bunch and that should help to keep 'em quiet and out of our hair.'

'In the meantime, we stick in town and run it as we figured, don't we?' one of the men asked. 'Don't fergit there's that town bank to be dealt with afore we go. Plenty in it worth havin' if we choose our time right.'

'Yeah, sure. We stick in town all right if only to show those dumb folks that we mean what we say.' Again Bannock fell to thought and his eyes narrowed a little. 'Mebbe I ain't finished with the dude an' Homburg just yet,' he said, 'anymore than they've finished with me. I'll show 'em somethin' afore I'm finished. Now let's git to the hotel and see what we can think up. I want a dry shirt for one thing.'

At this same moment Jane had just come to end of laying out a supper for Bart, his father, and herself. When they were all three seated Meredith began to explain his plan. 'We now know that Bannock is in this region for only one thing – to find gold. And in the course of trying it won't be long before he crosses swords with us again, as well as generally upsetting the peace of the community.'

'Right enough,' Bart agreed, eating hungrily meanwhile. 'But how long he'll be finding the gold Lord alone knows! We could be playing this cat-and-mouse business with him indefinitely, so I don't see how it solves our problem.'

'It would solve it completely,' Meredith smiled, 'if our unpleasant friends, in their search for gold, ran into a death trap!' Bart and Jane looked at him sharply. 'By nature, Son,' he continued, 'I am a peaceable man, but there are certain types of people for whom I have no regard whatever; those whom I would destroy as willingly as if they were a species of deadly insect. Bannock and his cohorts come into that class. Murderers, every one of them! Scum on the face of the earth!'

'All right, all right, so you don't like 'em,' Bart interrupted. 'If you've some new angle, let's have it.'

'Well, I thought it would be a novel notion to provide gold traces for the gentlemen to find. The said gold traces would actually be a bait which, I hope, would lead those men into a trap from which there would be very little chance of escape.'

Bart sighed and laid down his knife and fork in exasperation.

'You're still not making sense! Where on earth do you propose getting gold traces from, anyway? Start looking for the Wells-Fargo stuff yourself, do you mean? Or have you by some chance got secret information concerning a hidden gold mine?'

'Unfortunately not. As to the Wells-Fargo stuff itself, I shall of course search for it as time permits – but in the meantime I was thinking of using some pyrite rock, also known as iron sulphide. Its metallic yellow lustre is very attractive. I have several specimens in my room which I found in the foothills whilst out riding not long ago. I thought they might one day prove useful – and that day has now come!'

'Pyrite?' Bart repeated, frowning. 'Never heard of it.'

'But I have!' Jane exclaimed. 'It has a brass-yellow colour and is often mistaken for gold. In fact, it's known as Fool's Gold! But it may not be easy to fool Bannock with it, Randle. In the old days it led many a prospector to think he'd found a bonanza, but not any more. I can't quite see Bannock falling for it.'

Meredith ate for a while, then he gave his urbane grin. 'Before vetoing the idea, let us consider the moves he might make upon finding, or hearing of, traces of this substance. And I *will* make sure that he does hear of it. He would naturally have it analysed, and the only person to do that is Ron Milburn, the assayer for Mountain Peak.'

'Uh-huh,' Jane agreed. 'Logical so far.'

'Thank you, Jane. Now Mr Milburn is a law-abiding gentleman, I have found, and if I were to personally ask him to mislead our avaricious friend – for the good of the community – I've no doubt he'd be willing to deceive Bannock concerning pyrites if they were presented to him.'

'Well – maybe.' Bart rubbed his chin and looked doubtful. 'Supposing the deception came off, what would happen then?'

'Then, Son, assured that the stuff he had found was gold, Bannock would bend every effort with his men to dig near the spot where the traces were found. Get them nicely absorbed in that occupation – where they would no doubt also pitch a base camp – and then turn loose upon them a herd of some two thousand steers.'

102

'Do what?' Bart demanded, staring.

'Create a stampede, son, with two thousand head. Most unpleasant! If the outlaws are in a narrow canyon – as I will shall see to it they will be – they will not have much chance to escape and will be blotted out under the onslaught of flying hoofs if they cannot ride fast enough to get out of the way.'

'It sounds pretty horrible,' Jane said, with a little shiver. 'I've seen one or two stampedes in my time and believe me they are much more terrifying than you seem to imagine.'

'The more terrifying the better,' Meredith responded amiably. 'I have learned that out in this region the best thing for bad men is to have *accidents* happen to them until they are all eliminated just as an *accident* happened to Charlie. If these men were handed over to the authorities they would merely brazen things out and finish up by being hanged, or even just jailed. To men like them even hanging holds no particular terrors. They have lived the hard way and death does not frighten them.

'But,' Meredith continued, 'confront them with a horde of thundering destruction and for a few brief minutes as they race for their lives they will know something of the anguish they have brought to those they have killed in their foul careers – an anguish which ends in death. Which is as it should be.'

Meredith ceased talking and drank some coffee. His round, babyish face was without expression, the chubby lips set hard. Bart eyed him for a moment in the grim silence that had dropped.

Bart was recalling how, when he and his father had first came to Mountain Peak, they had found his brother's murdered body – victim of outlaws led by Jane's stepfather – who had himself since been hanged for his crimes. Bart reflected that the loss of his son had evidently affected his father more than he'd realized at the time.

'You're turning into quite a ruthless sort of devil, Dad!' he said quietly.

'No, Son, hardly that.'

'Sorry. It certainly looks that way from where I'm sitting. What do you think, Jane?'

Jane did not speak. She, like Bart, was recalling the recent tragic events. Instead, she gave a slow, reluctant nod. Meredith smiled inscrutably.

'It is simply that I am conforming to the requirements of the region in which I now live,' he explained. 'When it is a case of kill or be killed I am ruthless, yes – for make no mistake about it, Bannock will leave nothing unturned to eliminate you or me if he can. So the sooner he is taken care of, the better. In the morning I intend to survey the landscape to see if it is feasible to bring my plan to fruition. I want to examine every detail before I set the wheels moving.'

And he kept his word.

Immediately after breakfast the following morning, he set off on his stallion and rode by a roundabout route to Rocky Canyon. Everywhere he could take advantage of a fold in the landscape he did so, and though he remained constantly alert there was no sign of anybody in the whole vast waste of grass, loco-weed, and yucca.

Once he gained an arroyo he followed its twisting course until he came to the narrow cleft between the mountains – the cleft known locally as Rocky Canyon. Meredith drew rein presently at a spot where a lazy freshet trickled its way across sandy floor. Just here there were no flowers or vegetation, only the bare ground, spongy from the presence of the water, but not so spongy that pebbles had sunk into it.

Dismounting, Meredith reached into the saddle-bag and withdrew a chunk of yellow substance rather like coke, but far heavier.

With a piece of rock he managed finally to break it up into separate small pieces. These he tossed at random about the clearing near the freshet and watched for a moment to see that they did not sink.

Then he remounted the stallion and, taking care to avoid the clearing where the hoofprints would show, he circuited the course of the freshet and then continued on his way up the narrow cleft, Homburg hat on the back of his head, the sun beating torridly on his fleshy back.

'So far, so good, Hercules,' he commented, to the horse. 'I fancy that when our avaricious friends come upon those yellow lumps they will imagine they have struck what is popularly called a bonanza around these parts– Ah! Here is the view I wanted!' As if it had understood every word the beast obeyed. Taking care that he did not reveal himself against the skyline Meredith dismounted again to finish his journey on foot, leaving the horse to nibble at the few roots nearby. He emerged at the summit of the downwardly sloping canyon, well within the shadow of the giant spurs which marked its opening and gave the canyon its name. From here he was able to look out across rolling pastureland towards two distant ranches –

the Leaning-J and Bar-25, as he well knew.

'Excellent!' he murmured finally. 'With two thousand or so cattle stampeded through this canyon I imagine our dubious friends will have little, if any, chance ... and now to other matters.'

He remounted his stallion, and then took the risk of riding straight across the pasture-land to the distant Leaning-J. Apparently no gunmen were on the lookout in this deserted region for nothing happened.

Once at the ranch it did not take Meredith long to complete his mission. He left again with the promise of co-operation from the ranch-owner, obtained the same allegiance from the grizzled veteran who ran the Bar-25 outfit, and then he rode back to Rocky Canyon.

'Now, Hercules,' he murmured to the horse, as the animal plodded steadily through the giant fissure, 'we come to the more dangerous part. To visit the assayer I must of necessity go into town – and both you, my trusty steed, and I will be recognized. A little hard thinking is called for.'

After a while he smiled to himself, turned the horse's head, and set the animal speeding heavily in the direction of a third ranch some two miles distant nestling at the foot of the gigantic mountain range.

Fifteen minutes later, Meredith rode into the yard, dismounted, and lumbered his way up to the porch.

A big woman opened the screen-door to him and then gave a start of surprise.

'Well, if it ain't Mayor Meredith!'

Meredith beamed. 'Thank you, madam. It's rare for someone to remember my official designation these days!'

'Come right in, sir. I guess you haven't been around in some time and we're mighty glad to see you.'

Meredith followed her through the hall and into the sunny living-room where her husband – a lean, grey-haired rancher – was just finishing his breakfast.

'Howdy, Mayor,' he greeted, getting up and extending a bony brown hand. 'Nice to see you still in one piece and knocking around, considering the way John Bannock's been carrying on.'

'And still is,' the rancher's wife added, with a grim look. 'What d'you propose doing about that low-down jigger, Mr Mayor? Time he was taken care of, isn't it? I know you've bounced him around a bit, but that ain't enough. He wants a public hangin', nothing less.'

'Yes, madam, I agree,' Meredith said, settling his huge bulk in the wicker chair as the woman motioned to it. 'However, there are more ways of being rid of an outlaw than by hanging him. I have plans in mind for dealing with him, and because I am sure you are solidly behind me I am going to ask you for help.'

'Sure,' the grey-haired rancher said promptly. 'You only have to ask.'

'Splendid!' Meredith looked at the big, square-faced woman benevolently. 'Mrs Barlow, I would like to borrow from you a poke-bonnet, a pair of elastic-sided boots, an ankle-length dress – and a wagon and team. And perhaps a big shopping-basket.'

The woman looked at him in wonder. 'I don't mind supplyin' all them things, Mr Meredith, but what in heck d'you want 'em for?'

'I face a crisis, madam. For the further-ance of my scheme it's imperative that I visit the assayer in town. Were I to go as myself I would be committing suicide, hence the need of disguise. You and I are not dissimilar in the matter of – hmm – girth, madam, so I think the deception would be more or less foolproof.'

Satisfied with the explanation, the woman

109

nodded and hurried from the room. Her husband grinned.

'You sure choose some strange methods to get your way, Mr Mayor,' he commented. 'Care to explain?'

'Sorry,' Meredith responded, 'but my plans are more or less unformed at the moment. Just the basic details are worked out so far. I would remark, however, that if you should hear of any information concerning a gold strike it will be policy for you to ignore it. It will be entirely false.'

'Y'mean that Wells-Fargo gold which y'said in the Painted Lady last night Bannock and his men were lookin' for? That it?'

'Quite so.'

The rancher rubbed his chin. 'Well, OK. I'll ignore any rumours I hear, but I can't speak that way fur the rest of the folks.'

'Meaning?'

'Well, as I see it, plenty of 'em are already figurin' on diggin' up the landscape hereabouts to see what they can find – after what you said. Only I guess they'll have to do it in secret like.'

'Why in secret?'

'Because Bannock's threatened to shoot anybody who starts a-lookin'.'

'Just the kind of behaviour I might have

expected from our charming friend. Mmm – that probably accounts for the absence of eager prospectors. I expected to find the place more or less crawling with them...'

Meredith sat musing for a while, then he glanced up as the rancher's wife returned with a dress over her arm and a poke-bonnet and elastic-sided boots in her hand.

# 5

## A MAN FOR A MAN

'Here y'are, Mr Meredith! And y'can use the room back there if you want to change right now.'

'I do; and thank you, madam.'

Meredith rose and took the things from her, then he ambled ponderously to the adjoining room and closed the door. The rancher looked at it and grinned, then glanced at his still somewhat puzzled wife.

'Queer guy, ain't he?' he murmured.

'Sure is. Durned if I can figure some of the stunts he gets up to!'

'I'll go and fix the buckboard for him. He'll be needin' it next, I suppose.'

Five minutes later, Meredith emerged again, smiling amiably, the poke-bonnet encircling his face. The big woman looked at him steadily and then broke into a fleshy laugh, her hands on her hips.

'For land's sake, Mr Mayor, I never saw anythin' like it!' she declared. 'I guess you

113

look the best housewife I've seen around these parts in some time!'

'Yes indeed; quite fetching, am I not?' Meredith asked, beaming, and his round face and big blue eyes looked genuinely feminine with the softening effect of the poke-bonnet. 'Instead of any of Bannock's gunmen firing at me I'll probably have them helping me up the boardwalk steps! I will return the various articles to you the moment I have seen the assayer – and thank you again for your co-operation.'

As Meredith turned to the door the woman caught at his arm.

'Just a minute, Mr Mayor! You're not takin' a risk like this without a gun, are you?'

'Hardly, madam, hardly!'

Meredith reached inside the bosom of the dress and momentarily revealed his .45; then he buttoned up the dress again, smiled, and continued on his way outside.

He found the buckboard and team waiting for him, the rancher himself holding an enormous shopping basket.

'Best of luck, Mr Mayor,' he said, as he handed it over. 'I reckon you sure look the part if nothin' else.'

With a cherubic smile Meredith heaved his enormous body on to the driving seat;

then he said, 'I'll return for my stallion later. Please be good enough to stable him, just in case any of Bannock's men pass this way and recognize him. I'll also pick up my Homburg hat when I return, together with my boots and other odds and ends.'

With that Meredith started the team into action and drove non-stop into town, coming to a halt again in the main street a few yards from the assayer's. Removing the huge basket he clambered down from the buckboard and looked about him, using the shadow of the poke-bonnet to keep his face well shielded from the passers-by.

The main street was fairly busy, men and women going back and forth, and in and out of the various stores and offices, but none paid any particular attention to him. A fat housewife with a basket was the commonest sight possible in Mountain Peak, and there was certainly nothing to give away his sex and real identity.

Then Meredith's eyes narrowed as he recognized a 'puncher, advancing slowly along the boardwalk towards him, as one of Bannock's gunmen. He moved with the air of a sentry, one hand resting on the butt of his Colt.

Evidently the man was patrolling, alert for

the first sign of wrong moves on the part of the inhabitants – or, however unlikely, a visit from Bart or Meredith.

'Howdy, Ma!' he called, as he came nearer and Meredith lurched up the steps to the boardwalk, the basket over his arm. 'Grand mornin' for a bit of shoppin' huh? Need any help? Whilst we're runnin' this town we wants the folks – and specially the women – to feel comfortable.'

Meredith groped quickly in the pocket of the dress and dragged out a white hand-kerchief. 'That's a good one,' he murmured; then he put the handkerchief to his face and pitched his voice to its highest treble. 'Better keep away from me, feller,' he cautioned. 'I've gotten the worst cold you ever did see. Always do at this time of the year. Dust, I reckon.'

The gunman grinned. 'Colds don't worry me, Ma. And how's about me carryin' that basket for you when you get it loaded?'

'Why should you?' Meredith snapped. 'Don't I look strong enough to do me own carryin'?'

'Oh yeah, sure you do. Only tryin' to help – boss's orders.'

'Mighty strange orders for a man who's started gun-law,' Meredith observed.

'Shucks, Ma, you shouldn't believe all you hear. Just a matter of keepin' things neat and tidy, and sometimes a gun's the only way to do it.'

'That so?' Meredith asked grimly. 'Well, I reckon that Mayor Meredith and his sheriff son'll teach you boys somethin' afore you're much older.'

'Shouldn't be at all surprised,' the gunman agreed drily.

'You can take the word of an old woman on that,' Meredith added. 'I get around I do, and see things.' He sniffed and pulled the handkerchief higher.

'Yeah?' the gunman asked sharply. 'You know somethin' more than the rest of us, Ma?'

'All I do know is that as I rode this way I saw the mayor and the sheriff busy in Rocky Canyon. What doin' I don't know. Mebbe lookin' for that gold Bannock won't let any of us start searchin' for.'

'Yeah? That's mighty interestin', Ma. What more do you know?'

'I don't know any more than that. I've said all I'm goin' to.'

Rather than risk saying anything more Meredith turned away and lumbered into the general stores. After a studied survey of the shelves he bought a variety of items that could be used at the Slanting-F, and whilst he made his selection he watched the gunman outside. For a time the man stood thinking, rubbing his stubbly chin; then evidently coming to a decision he turned and headed away along the boardwalk.

'Splendid!' Meredith muttered. 'If he does what I think he'll do that saves me a lot of trouble. This chance meeting has given me the way to tempt the outlaws into the canyon, there to the Fool's Gold. Amazing how completely gullible these tough he-men of the West can be!'

He completed his purchases and escaped before the obviously somewhat curious store-dealer – unable to place having seen his customer before – could have time to ask questions.

His loaded basket on his arm, Meredith went on to the boardwalk and looked about him. To his relief the parading gunman had disappeared, and indeed was probably closeted somewhere with John Bannock.

Meredith covered the brief distance to the assayer's office and glided inside. Reaching the counter set at right-angles to a high wooden partition he banged his fist upon it. Behind the partition there were sounds of movement, then a scrawny man with a sunken face and grey hair wearing steel-rimmed spectacles came into view.

He latched his thumbs in his vest pockets and peered at his customer over the tops of his spectacles.

'Somethin' I can do for you, ma'am'?'

'I am delighted that you should be deluded in regard to my sex, Mr Milburn,' Meredith beamed, and spoke in his normal voice. 'Don't you recognize me?'

'Durn me, if it ain't Mayor Meredith!' the assayer exclaimed, his mouth gaping. 'What in Sam Hill are you gotten up like that for?'

'Disguise, my dear sir – obviously. I am here on urgent business and I must get it over as quickly as possible.' Meredith leaned confidentially over the counter. 'It is conceivable, Mr Milburn, that before long one of Bannock's men – or even Bannock himself – may bring to you some yellow metal resembling gold, for the purpose of having it analysed. It will actually be Fool's Gold – pyrite, the interesting properties of which I hardly need inform you. Now, sir, you can do the community a service if you inform whoever brings in the stuff that it is genuine gold.'

'I can?' The assayer reflected for a while,

then smiled tightly. 'What you mean is, you're tryin' to pull somethin' on these no-account heels who are doin' their best to try and run the town?'

'Doing their worst, Mr Milburn, would be more apt. Yes, that is the situation exactly, the crux of my plan relying upon your giving a false analysis. You *must* say that the stuff is gold, at all costs. Your word as an assayer will never be questioned for a moment, no matter how much the stuff may resemble iron sulphide.'

'I guess you're right, Mr Mayor. Pyrites and gold are enough alike to fool anyone who isn't an expert. But what's the set-up behind it?'

'That's too long a story to explain here. But I promise you the outcome should mean the end of those gunmen.'

The assayer grinned.

'To give them something to sweat about, Mr Mayor, I'll do anythin'!'

'Excellent. I'll leave it to you. Now I must be on my way.'

Meredith headed for the door, basket on his arm, and looked about him cautiously on gaining the boardwalk. Things were still more or less peaceful. He reached the buckboard, and placed his basket within it, then in a few minutes he was on his way back down the trail.

He was resolved that as he returned from the Barlows' ranch to the Slanting-F, he would see if anything was transpiring in Rocky Canyon. If so he would be reasonably sure that the rest of his plan could be brought to success.

Bannock was riding hard across the pasture-land from Mountain Peak, two of his men beside him.

'If this turns out to be a bum steer you've handed me, Hank, I'll damn well crown you! I've heard some of your fancy tales before!'

'I ain't takin' no responsibility, boss,' Hank retorted defensively. 'That old dame said Homburg and his dude son were up to somethin' in Rocky Canyon – and that's all I know. But it could be they've found that gold we're lookin' for. You said it was probably somewhere around that canyon.'

'Just give me a chance to get a crack at 'em where they can't hit back!' Bannock muttered, his eyes glinting. 'Mebbe I can pick them off from behind a rock. That fat guy's a tricky swine to deal with in the open. Seems to be quicker with his noodle than his son.'

He became silent again, digging in the

spurs and hurtling his mount across the grass, then over the sandy waste with its outcroppings of scrub that marked the base of the foothills. Here he began to slow down his mount somewhat, realizing the necessity for caution.

Making scarcely any sound, he and his two colleagues plodded their horses through the arid dust and sand following an arroyo, watching ahead keenly for the first signs of trouble. Nothing presented itself. The landscape was deserted.

'Looks like that old dame was havin' you on a string, Hank,' Bannock commented, as they came within sight of the canyon.

'No reason why she should, Jack. I figured she knew what she was talkin' about.'

'Then where the hell are they?'

'Mebbe they just left,' Hank responded. 'Ain't nothin' so unusual about that, is there?'

Bannock grunted, then he transferred his attention to the looming rocks about them, contemplating the crags and pinnacles reaching peak and dome into the sky. His hand remained on his gun in readiness for any attack, but nothing happened.

'There's been a horse, or horses, around here anyways,' the second man said abruptly, pointing to the ground a few yards from the freshet. 'Look at them prints! They're only just visible but they ain't been made long – and from the look of 'em it was a mighty big cayuse which made 'em.'

Bannock drew to a halt and looked at the ground with a studied intentness.

'Yeah, Sam, you're right,' he admitted at length. 'And there's only one horse that could make prints like that, I reckon – that big stallion Homburg always rides. Mebbe that old woman weren't stringin' you along after all, Hank – though how in blue thunder she even got as far as this canyon is something I can't quite make out. I wonder if she was... Hey, take a look!' Bannock broke off sharply.

He pointed ahead, then he slid quickly from the saddle and hurried over to where he had caught the light of something gleaming in the sun. In a moment or two he had the chunk of pyrite rock in his palm and tossed it up and down experimentally.

Hank came hurrying over to him, his face startled. He stared at the stuff fixedly.

'Hell's bells, Jack, that's gold!'

'Mebbe.' Bannock looked at the stuff carefully. 'Mebbe it is gold and mebbe it ain't,' he responded. 'That Wells-Fargo stuff would be in blocks, not loose chunks like this seems to be. And come to think of it, not in blocks either,' he added, pondering. 'Bricks. Gold bricks. If this stuff is gold the only explanation is that it belongs to a brick that got dropped or smashed somehow, and this is a lump from it...'

'There's more here!' Sam cried, and came racing over with two small bits of the stuff in his leathery palm.

Bannock looked at it for a while and then his eyes narrowed, and he looked about him.

'Somethin' wrong?' Sam asked in surprise. 'Looks to me as though we've happened on somethin' worth havin', Jack.'

'Either there's somethin' mighty screwy goin' on around here, or else we ain't far from that Wells-Fargo stuff – else a bonanza of some kind,' Bannock decided. 'The part I don't like is that Dude and Homburg have been here before us. I'm wonderin' if they found the darned stuff, took it away, and happened to drop these bits as they did it.'

The three men looked at one another morosely, inwardly savage at the thought of perhaps having been cheated of their prize by the two men they hated most. Then all of a sudden Hank gave a yelp and pointed high above them.

'Homburg!' he yelled, dragging out his gun. 'Watchin' us! Look, boss!'

At the same instant Bannock and Sam saw the figure of Meredith distinctly – or at least his unmistakable head and shoulders and the Homburg hat. But even as Hank's bullet whanged upwards to a point fifty feet above, the brief vision of Meredith vanished. Infuriated, Bannock fired too – then he stopped and swore.

'Him all right,' he muttered, hesitating.

'What in heck's the matter with us?' Hank snapped. 'Why don't we git after him and quick.'

'Wouldn't be no use, Hank. There ain't nothin' we can do about it. We'd never reach that high rimrock in under half an hour.' Bannock rubbed his chin as he stood puzzling things out. 'I just don't git the hang of this set-up at all... I guess we'd better go back into town and take some of this stuff with us; then we can see if it's gold. If it is we're goin' to git busy in this canyon, with two of us on the watch for Dude and Homburg. That old woman was right, Hank. Seems pretty certain that Homburg was watchin' us all the time.'

'Yeah...' Hank frowned as he holstered his

gun. 'Wonder why he didn't shoot us? He had the complete drop on us!'

'I guess you can thank his conscience for that,' Bannock grinned sourly. 'He's the sort of mug who believes it ain't right to plug a guy when he ain't lookin'. OK, let's git back into town.'

Meredith arrived back at the Slanting-F just after noon and, after watering and stabling the stallion, he carried his groceries into the ranch by the back door and then made his way into the living-room.

Bart and Jane, in their working overalls, were having lunch and they looked up expectantly. 'From the look in your eye, Randle, you've been up to plenty.' Jane commented. 'Sit down. Everything's ready for you to start eating.'

Meredith settled in a chair and then dabbed his forehead gently. 'I had rather a narrow escape upon my return here and rode faster than normally. I found it quite an exertion – for a man of my weight.'

He took a long drink of raspberry wine and then settled back, his normal beatific smile coming to his moonlike countenance.

'I have had a most intriguing morning, even to the extent of disguising myself as a

126

cross between Mrs Grundy and Old Mother Hubbard!'

'You what?' Jane asked blankly.

Meredith smiled and began to explain in detail. By the time he had finished, speaking in his usual roundabout fashion, he was also half way through his lunch.

'...and on the way home,' he concluded, 'I detoured to Rocky Canyon to see if the sprat had caught the whale. It certainly had! I had only been in my lofty eyrie for a few minutes when Bannock and two of his men arrived. As I had hoped it was not long before they were examining the gold nuggets – otherwise pyrite. It was just at that moment, however, that they caught sight of me.'

'What happened?' Jane asked anxiously.

'They fired – but since I was at such a height and distance from them they missed completely. Do not imagine, however, that my revealing myself was accidental.'

'But why on earth should you have wanted them to see you?' Bart demanded.

'Purely to satisfy our friends that the "old woman" in town spoke the truth! I imagine they are too dim-witted to realize that the woman might have been me – particularly after seeing me on the rimrock such a short time afterwards. My plan relies on them not suspecting anything.'

'It all seems damned involved to me, Dad,' Bart sighed. 'But remembering what you said about making them suffer before they die I suppose it's justified. And you say everything's fixed up at the Leaning-J and Bar-25 spreads for you to get busy on the stampede?'

'Everything, son – two thousand head of them – but before that can occur we have to be sure that Bannock and his men are nicely based in the canyon, otherwise the whole business will be a waste of time. When we do act it will of course be at night.'

Bart nodded. 'All right, then. That means that one or other of us will have to keep a constant watch on the canyon, I take it?'

'Yes, and naturally whichever of us is on guard must take exquisite care not to be seen. I propose to take the first period on watch immediately after lunch, you to relieve me after an interval of three hours, if you will?'

'OK,' Bart agreed. 'That will give me plenty of time during the afternoon to get a few things straightened up around the spread. Ordinary work has to go on, Bannock and his men notwithstanding.'

Meredith nodded complacently and con-

128

tinued with his meal – about which time Bannock and his men were riding back into Mountain Peak. Detailing his men to their usual points for guard duty, the outlaw took it on himself to stride into the assayer's office and, unknown to that bespectacled gentleman behind the partition, Bannock also took the precaution to slip the bolt across the outer door.

'Hey you!' he commanded, banging on the counter. 'Jump to it! I've some stuff here I want examining.'

Ron Milburn came into view at that, peering over his steel-rimmed spectacles. He was too mature a man to betray in the slightest that he was surprised to see the outlaw standing there so soon after the visit from Meredith.

'Well?' he asked, uncompromisingly.

'Here – examine this and tell me what it is.'

The assayer looked at the chunk of yellow metal, which fell heavily on the counter. He picked it up and peered at it; then he went behind the partition for a while. Presently he returned and laid the stuff on the counter again.

'It's gold.' he said briefly. 'Around ten carat.'

'Sure?' Bannock's voice was suspicious but Milburn met his glare steadily.

'There wouldn't be much point in me sayin' it's gold if it isn't, would there? Sure it is, and it wouldn't surprise me if it don't belong to that Wells-Fargo stuff which the mayor was talkin' about in the saloon last night.'

Bannock grinned unpleasantly and cuffed up his hat.

'You're doin' everythin' except ask me right out where I found the stuff ain't you?' he asked.

'It doesn't really matter to—'

'Shut up while I'm talkin'! The moment my back's turned you'll start huntin' for it yourself, and you'd tell others what I brought in here.'

The assayer shook his grey head.

'I'm not that kind of a man, Bannock. I run my business by respectin' the confidence of those who come in here. Hell, if I didn't I'd be startin' gold rushes and stampedes every other day!'

'Yeah? Well there's one you sure ain't goin' to start this time, feller! I'm not leavin' you around to tell anybody that you know I've found gold....'

Too late, the assayer dived at his gun im-

130

mediately below the counter. Before he could grasp it Bannock's .45 blurred upward from the holster and fired point-blank. Grim-faced, he watched the assayer slowly crumple and then become motionless on the other side of the counter.

Bannock returned the gun to his holster, turned to the door; unlocked it, and peered outside. At the moment there was nobody within a hundred yards, and they were not looking in his direction – so he inserted himself casually on to the boardwalk and closed the door behind him. Satisfied that he had not been observed leaving – and quite sure that nobody had seen him enter – he ambled along the boardwalk until he came to the spot where Hank was perched on the hitch rail, smoking and keeping a keen look-out on the populace.

'It's gold,' Bannock said, lighting a cigarette for himself and then contemplating the main Street. 'Around ten carat. That no-account chiseller told me as much and I don't reckon he'd have any reason for lyin'.'

'Then...' Hank's eyes brightened. 'Mebbe there's a whole lot of that Wells-Fargo stuff up in the canyon, boss! We'd best go and look, hadn't we?'

'That's what we're goin' to do, and that

guy Milburn won't be tellin' anybody anythin' either. All he needs right now is a lily on his chest.'

Hank looked dubious. 'Was rubbin' him out a good idea, boss? The folks around here thought quite a lot of Milburn. He was the only guy in town who could do any analysing when any dirt-washer happened on to somethin' worth havin' – and the only guy who could value it and turn it into cash. They ain't goin' to be pleased about his death.'

'You think I was goin' to take the risk of lettin' him shout his face off do you? Anyway, nobody knows I bumped him off: they can only think it and that don't do 'em any good at all. Right now we've things to do, Hank. We need full equipment to pitch a camp in that canyon, then we'll go over it with a toothcomb, see, and try and trace where that Wells-Fargo stuff is hidden.'

'And suppose Dude and Homburg have already taken it?'

Bannock brooded for a while, smoking slowly. Then he gave a shrug.

'Well, if they have they couldn't have done it without leavin' traces – 'specially the marks of horses' hoofs. Those we found came from the scrubland and the stuff sure wasn't hidden there. What we've got to do is search the foothills all through the canyon. And if we do find traces showin' that them two have gotten there first we'll go right to their spread and shoot it out with 'em. That's the set-up, and think yourself lucky, Hank, that I'm lettin' you and the boys in on this.'

'Lucky nothin',' Hank returned sourly. 'You know durned well you can't search for the stuff by yourself! OK – when do we go?'

'Right now. Get the boys. We'll have to risk leavin' the town to its own devices for a while. Meet me at the general store. I'm going to grab some provender for ourselves and the cayuses. We may have to be away some time.'

Hank nodded and set off up the boardwalk. Bannock went in the opposite direction, to the general store. In ten minutes he had got all he needed – without paying for it, as usual – and with his four men to help him he loaded up the horses. Then they set off together up the main street and soon vanished in a cloud of whirling dust.

Meredith, perched high on the rimrock overlooking Rocky Canyon, was smoking a cheroot and lazily considering the valley below when he first caught sight of the five

133

horsemen from the plume of dust they had raised in the dusty foothills.

Immediately he became alert and picked up a pair of field-glasses from beside him. He was able to follow the progress of the men with ease, taking care that he remained in a niche between two high pinnacles where he could not possibly be seen. The only person who would be able to find him was Bart, who knew exactly the spot that had been chosen.

Meredith lowered the glasses and with naked eye watched the men halt fifty feet below and glance about them intently. They even looked straight towards him, failed to discern the slit through which he was peering, and then they dismounted and set about the task of unloading their horses. By degrees a tent was erected, then followed cooking utensils, spades, and various odds and ends. The horses were hobbled together a little distance away where they could chew at the nearest roots.

'Lambs to the slaughter,' Meredith murmured. 'I'll be able to put my master-plan into operation tonight!'

He sat watching for another half-hour and by this time the outlaws had made their camp in the centre of a ring of thorny ocotillo bushes, presumably to keep away any prowling mountain cats during the night hours. This task completed they set about a meal, the five of them squatting beside a camp-fire which they kept well ablaze to prevent heavy smoke giving away its position.

At a sudden sound, Meredith started and dropped his hand to the rifle he had brought with him; then he found himself looking up at Bart as he crawled into view amidst the rocks.

'I had the hell of a job finding you, Dad.'

'Sorry, Son – but the more complicated the route to this eyrie, the better. However, the geese are just fattening themselves nicely for the slaughter...'

Bart peered through the niche between the rocks and then gave a nod. He squatted down at his father's side and cuffed his sombrero up on to his forehead.

'I've put my horse near yours, Dad – in that little clearing, where with any luck it shouldn't be seen. And I've also got some news for you.'

'What news, Son?'

'Just before I left the spread Ken Bradman came riding in from town – he's the town's druggist, remember? Seems he wanted you and me right away to see the body of Ron

Milburn, the assayer. He's been shot dead. It's my job as sheriff to view the body and make a report on the circumstances attending the death, so the authorities in Wilson City can know all about it. Your job is to say what should be done in regard to disposing of the corpse and informing the victim's relatives, if any. Far as I know there aren't any in this case.'

Meredith compressed his lips. 'I suppose I should have expected something like that, but I didn't. It never occurred to me that he might be risking his life. Who did the shooting? Bannock?'

'There seems little doubt of it. Milburn probably analysed the pyrite and stated that it was gold – as you had asked him to – and to prevent others from getting the information, Bannock then shot Milburn dead. We might have known!'

Meredith brooded for a while, clearly troubled; then he began to look somewhat puzzled. 'If Ken Bradman rode in from the town, that would suggest that the town is no longer guarded, otherwise he would likely have been stopped.'

Bart nodded. 'He did say that Bannock and his boys had departed so he took the chance of coming after us. Since the outlaws

136

are down there in the canyon the explanation is simple. The point we've got to clear up is: what do we do about Milburn?'

'There's nothing we can do, as far as going into town and doing things officially is concerned. But we'll certainly take care of one of Bannock's boys in reprisal, as I warned them I would. A man for a man, son, every time!'

'Which gives you the legal right to shoot Bannock himself and have done with it,' Bart said.

'It doesn't, I'm afraid. We don't know for certain that it was he who shot Milburn. That's immaterial just as long as one of that cut-throat gang is destroyed. They'll never learn any other way.'

Bart wriggled up and peered at the five men round their camp-fire in the valley below. They were in the shadow now apparently cooking a meal. The late afternoon sun was already dipping behind the mountain range.

'If you're planning to wipe the lot of them out later on, why bother to blot out just one now? You'll give away your position, too.'

'That can't be helped. And remember that there's no guarantee that every one of those men will be killed in the stampede, if they ride fast enough to escape. In that way I feel they are given a chance. So one of them has got to be dealt with in order that my promise of reprisal can be carried out. Giving away our position hardly signifies. Those men will not leave their camp down there until they have made every effort to find what they believe is gold – but they certainly will come gunning for us.'

'Then we'll have to get out of here quickly. So how are we supposed to keep track of their movements once we've lost this hiding place?'

'We won't need to,' Meredith responded. 'We can take it for granted that they will remain here for some time to come. Tonight we'll act and release the stampede … meantime, I have a short message to write.'

He tugged a scratch-pad from his pocket and with a stump of a pencil wrote a message in block capitals. When he had finished he handed the sheet to Bart.

RONALD MILBURN
DEMANDS VENGEANCE.

A MAN FOR A MAN.

'OK,' Bart acknowledged. 'That should let

them know what's coming, anyway.'

Meredith took the note back and then picked up a heavy chunk of rock. He fixed the note, folded, in a tight crack of the rock. Then he raised himself, measured the distance with his eye to the men below, and withdrew as quickly as he sent the rock hurtling down. It landed only a few feet from Bannock himself.

He looked about him sharply, obviously startled. His gun was glinting in his hand in readiness. Getting up, he went over to the rock and examined it. Watching him intently through the niche in the rocks Bart and his father saw him hurry back to his men. Drawing their guns, they all got to their feet, and looked at the frowning canyon walls about them.

'Many a time those cut-throats have put innocent victims on the spot, none of them knowing from where or when death would strike them down,' Meredith said, with a hard smile. 'Now they are in a similar plight themselves, and not at all enjoying it! They know we are near at hand, but cannot detect where.'

'They'll know fast enough when you fire.'

'Quite so – but long before they can reach this spot we shall be away.'

Meredith waited for a further few minutes, smiling at the sight of the men darting wary glances about them, their guns at the ready. Then he reached down and picked up the rifle, resting it in the niche between the rocks and peering with one round blue eye down the barrel. The end of it ranged over each man and settled finally on Hank, standing a little apart from the others.

'Did it ever occur to you how the West gives a man a feeling of power? The law around these parts is so lax that with a rifle in one's hands one has the feeling of omniscience. My finger alone is the dividing line between life and death for our unspeakable friend Hank, who at the moment is right in the sights.'

'Look, Dad, suppose he wasn't the one who shot Milburn? That wouldn't be justice.'

'I beg to differ. We know from the reward notices that he has shot many other people, so the exact identity of the victim for whom he is paying the ultimate price does not signify. Besides, from the personal standpoint I detest him, and for another I do not wish Bannock to have a quick, comfortable exit from a bullet. So – here goes!'

Meredith pressed the trigger.

The rifle kicked back against his big shoulder and the explosion of the shot rippled back in diminishing echoes from the canyon walls. A split second after the whang of the bullet, Hank dropped and lay still. Bannock and his three remaining companions rushed in upon him, then almost as quickly a hail of revolver shots came from them up towards the fissure.

'Out, Son – quickly!' Meredith instructed, keeping low and darting forward.

# 6

## STAMPEDE

In twenty minutes, unscathed, Meredith and Bart were back at the Slanting-F. Jane looked at them in surprise as they came into the living-room.

'Something go wrong?' she enquired. 'I thought you were taking over for your father, Bart.'

'I was, but there's been a change of plan. We thought we'd better get back here in readiness to defend ourselves if need be...' and Bart added the details of that which had happened.

'I don't altogether agree with your ruthless methods, Randle,' Jane said. 'It sounds to me as though you are slowly becoming as hardened a gunman as most men of the West. It's – a bit of a shock, too.'

'Perhaps I am, Jane,' Meredith admitted, with his beatific smile. 'After all, when in Rome do as the Romans do. This business has developed into more or less of a shooting match between Bannock and his gunhawks and ourselves, and I intend to see that we win. Since the official notice says "dead or alive" for all those men, I am well within my rights in shooting them.'

'Well – perhaps so.'

Jane gave a little shrug. Her essentially feminine nature was still a trifle appalled, but she let the matter drop. Then Bart asked his father a question.

'Do you think they'll come here gunning for us?'

'It's unlikely they'll risk that.' Meredith shook his head. 'They will have sense enough to know that we shall be expecting them and ready to snipe them off as they approach. They'll wait until they get a chance for the odds to be less heavily weighed against them – but since tonight should see the end of them, that chance is not likely to materialize.'

Meredith laid the rifle on the table, considered, then continued.

'All we have to do is wait until nightfall and then ride out to the Bar-25 and Leaning-J and get the stampede under way. Under the cover of night we'll be safe enough and moonrise will not be until the early hours. Before we do arrange the stampede we shall of course make sure our friends are still in the canyon, as I expect they will.'

And on that note matters rested for the time being.

Meredith had guessed correctly: there was no sign of Bannock or any of his men making a direct reprisal on the ranch. So, after a late evening meal, as the brief twilight settled into dusk, the two men made ready, their guns strapped down to each thigh and Meredith carrying his field-glasses over his shoulder.

'Frankly, I find this life much more interesting than the paperwork associated with my old import business back in Boston,' he commented, smiling. 'Shooting it out with desperadoes is, to my mind, extremely stimulating.'

'And dangerous,' Bart reminded him grimly, as Jane lighted the oil lamp. 'Not that I mind for myself: I relish it as much as you do. But what about leaving Jane here?' He glanced at his wife. 'We did it once before, and you know what happened!'

'I was unprepared on that occasion,' she answered quickly. 'This time, with our three boys posted to constantly watch the spread at different points, and me here with my gun ready on the table, I should be safe.'

'Yes, that should be enough,' Meredith

agreed, and then cast a glance at the darkened window. 'Time to be on our way, and I would suggest, Jane, that you do not use the oil lamp. It's something of a give-away.'

Jane nodded, cupped her hand round the chimney glass, and blew out the flame. Then she went with the two men to the porch and watched them mount their horses.

'No telling when we'll be back,' Bart said, as he stooped and kissed her. 'Just look after yourself, that's all. The boys know exactly what to do. They're all posted.'

'I will,' Jane promised, and then she stood watching as the two men rode off across the yard and into the dim uncertainty of the starlight.

Knowing exactly what their plan was both men rode on in silence, heading for Rocky Canyon by the roundabout route between high-rising folds of land so that they wouldn't be seen appearing against the skyline.

In twenty minutes they had reached the lower foothills and began to follow the dimly marked acclivity, which led to the point where, formerly, Meredith had made his eyrie. They did not go right to it, however – in case Bannock or one of his gunmen might be there in readiness – but instead branched off a mile from it and sent the horses struggling up rocky slopes until finally they gained the further end of the rimrock. Here, well concealed by the towering spurs and darkness, they could gaze down on the canyon unhindered.

It took them some little time to accustom their eyes, but at length they could descry some distance away a dim red spot and about it a roughly designed dark square. Meredith tugged out his glasses and focused them.

In the lenses, the red spot became a carefully shielded camp-fire, the redness coming from the glowing ash under the grate the gunmen had built up of rocks. Meredith felt sure that the dark outlines belonged to the camping equipment, and possibly the sprawled men themselves.

'They're there all right,' he said, handing over the glasses.

Bart took them, peered intently for a while, then nodded. 'Just waiting for it. OK, we'd better be on our way to the Bar-25 and Leaning-J. Let's go.'

They turned their horses' heads round and began the descent of the rocks, quite satisfied in their own minds that Bannock was not attempting any reprisal as yet for the shooting of Hank. Perhaps the shot had not even been fatal; there was no way of knowing at the moment.

But, for once, both Meredith and his son had accepted too much at face value. At this very moment a shadowy figure was outside the fence of the Slanting-F's main yard, moving low down, silent, his dark clothes and the black kerchief up to his eyes destroying all outline. Some distance away his horse was reined to a broken tree stump.

John Bannock had in fact only been a few yards from the ranch since twilight had fallen. Full length behind an up-thrusting piece of land, topped by a solitary manzanita thicket it had been easy for him to watch whatever happened at the Slanting-F. He had seen the two depart, even heard the words as they had taken leave of the girl. Now the ranch was silent and in darkness, Jane still leaving the oil lamp extinguished.

Bannock grinned coldly to himself. Some-where – according to what he had overheard Bart say – there were men posted. His task was to get them all in a group and then deal with them. This was not a particularly tough job for a man of Bannock's criminal calibre.

He glided towards the main gateway and within throwing distance of the nearest corral where the cattle were silent at the moment

148

under the stars. To pick up a heavy chunk of stone and hurl it amidst them was only a moment's work, but the uproar it started was immediate. Somewhere a steer howled dismally as it was hit and, in sympathy, the other animals took up the chorus.

Within seconds, three men came from the shadows cloistering the ranch and went over to the corral. They held a quick consultation, which Bannock could not overhear and then went into the corral to investigate the cause of the trouble.

Immediately the outlaw seized his chance to speed across the yard, but he did not immediately make for the ranch house. Instead he came to a halt within the shadow of the outhouses no more than a few yards from the main corral gate through which the men had gone. Whilst he waited, quite invisible, he uncoiled a lariat from about his waist, prepared it with an extra large noose and stood with it hanging slackly in his right hand.

Gradually the noise of the disturbed cattle ceased and Bannock became more alert. A few minutes later, the three men came into view again, one behind the other, and passed through the gateway, locking the gate after them.

Bannock measured his distance then flung the rope and drew it tight simultaneously. He was too experienced at the game to miss over such a short distance. The tug he gave tightened the big noose round all three men and jammed them together. The jolt backwards he gave made it impossible for them to aim their guns even though they knew the direction from which the rope was being pulled.

His own gun levelled, Bannock came out of seclusion.

'Take it easy!' he commanded. 'Drop your guns!'

The men obeyed. Securely bound to each other as they were, back to back, there was nothing else they could do. Working with one hand the outlaw threw the guns away, then with the remaining length of rope he knotted it round the men's ankles, took the kerchief of each one and made it into a gag. Finally, with a shove he knocked them over helplessly in a body where they lay at the foot of the corral fence.

'That should hold you for a while,' he said drily, as he saw them glaring up at him. 'Meanwhile I've got things to do.'

He left the men and went across to the ranch house. He did not attempt the front door knowing that that would give the girl far too much time in which to act, and probably lose him his advantage. Instead, he crept round to the three windows, which he judged belonged to the main living-room. Pausing at the centre one he smashed his revolver barrel through it and then ducked down again, waiting. As he had expected Jane came to it almost immediately and opened it, looking out into the night.

'Larry! Bob!' she called. 'Did you throw something?'

'I did,' Bannock answered curtly, straightening. 'Take it easy if you want to go on livin'.'

Instantly Jane tried to dodge back, but she was not quick enough. Bannock's hand seized her right wrist, twisted the gun from her fingers, and then held her firmly.

'Out you get!' he snapped. 'Make it quick!'

Jane tried again to drag back, until realizing the futility of it she had to obey. She scrambled through the window frame and Bannock caught her as she dropped.

'Yell if you want,' he said grimly, his gun in her back. 'Your men are hog-tied and your husband and pot-belly are too far off to hear you. I don't know where they've gone but I reckon Rocky Canyon's as good a guess as any.'

'I'm not telling you where they've gone!' Jane retorted, as she was forced relentlessly across the yard. 'And this second snatch won't do you any good. You–'

'Aw, shut up, you stupid dame!' Abruptly Bannock whipped off his kerchief with his free hand and wound it round the girl's face, taking care to draw it tight between her teeth. Though he had to holster his gun whilst he knotted the kerchief securely the relaxation was of no use to Jane.

She no longer had her own gun and certainly not the strength to fight the iron-muscled outlaw. So, compelled to be silent, she walked on across the yard and finally to where Bannock's horse was standing reined to the broken tree stump.

'Git up in that saddle!' Bannock ordered; but he had to lift the girl to it bodily before he got obedience. This done, he tied her hands to the saddlehorn; then he leapt up behind her and spurred the animal into violent activity, sending it hurtling across the starlit pastureland in the direction of the dim bulk of the mountains.

'I've a good reason for this snatch,' Bannock said, as the horse galloped along. 'I reckon that your husband and Homburg know where there's gold hidden and aim to take it, some of which they've probably taken already. You'll know where it is – that lily-white husband of yours seems like the type who'd tell his wife everythin'.'

Jane mumbled something behind the gagging kerchief.

'Once I've learned all I want from you, sweetheart, I'm going to kill you! No trimmings, no nothin' – just a bullet through your little heart. Then I'll return your body to your husband somehow. I guess that'll learn him to go around pickin' off my men when they can't defend themselves. He got Hank today – or else Homburg did – and it's time there was some sort of an answer to that. You're it – and before you die you'll talk, or suffer! Please yourself.'

Jane bit savagely at the gag but there were no words she could utter. Now she knew where she was going her consternation was complete – not just because of the outlaw's threats, but because she could not speak of the stampede which was threatening, and in which she herself would inevitably be involved unless she were allowed to say half a dozen words. But apparently the outlaw had no intention of removing the gag yet, and after a moment or two he explained why.

'It won't be long, sister, afore we reach

Rocky Canyon where I've got a base camp. If your husband and Homburg ain't been taken care of by the boys I left on watch it's a cinch they'll be some place handy. One scream from you might blow things sky-high...'

Jane writhed in the saddle, struggling to free her securely knotted wrists from the saddlehorn, but it was a useless effort. She relaxed again, gazing anxiously ahead as the outlaw now rode his horse into the foothills, looking anxiously about him for a sign of attack.

But no attack came since, as the girl knew, if everything had gone according to plan, Bart and his father would be at the Leaning-J and Bar-25 getting ready for the cattle stampede. They would also be unaware that she would be right in its track.

Ten minutes of climbing amidst the rough stones of the acclivity brought the horse to the canyon itself. It moved with more ease now speeding towards the dimly visible glow at the base of the camp-fire. Three men stood in the shadows with guns ready until Bannock's voice satisfied them as to his identity.

Drawing to a halt, he untied the girl's hands from the horn but kept her wrists secured. Then he set her on her feet and nudged her forward. In a moment or two she had reached the centre of the camp, the men watching her narrowly in the dim starlight.

'Anythin' more happened, Mike?' Bannock asked the nearest man briefly.

'Not a thing, Jack.'

'That's damned queer,' the outlaw muttered. 'I saw Homburg and the dude leave their spread long ago, and I could have sworn they'd come here for you to deal with 'em.'

'We ain't seen 'em,' Mike commented.

'Then they must have seen this camp-fire from above and are watchin' – mebbe figurin' out whether they can shoot straight in the starlight. And you've a durned sight too much fire showin',' the outlaw added bluntly. 'Put some more rocks round the base of it.'

As this was done, Jane glanced anxiously about her, listening too for the first sounds that would signify the approach of the stampeded herd down the canyon. When that happened she had no doubt but what Bannock and his boys would ride like the devil and leave her to be crushed to death. She could run, certainly, since her feet were still untied, but...

Then even this possibility vanished as

Bannock stooped and drew a cord tight about her ankles. After that a shove knocked her over on her back where she remained, gazing at the outlaw's big figure outlined against the stars.

'I don't have to tell you, sweetheart, that I ain't the sentimental type,' he said grimly. 'I want some information from you. Right here I've got a whip...'

He raised it from the darkness of the odds and ends that formed the camp and Jane saw its twisted tail dangling against the stars.

'I'm goin' to use it on you until you nod your head. When you nod it means you know where that gold is and are willin' to take me to it. I'm not ungaggin' you till then because I want your screams stifled – they could bring shots down on us. This is goin' to hurt plenty, unless you're ready to talk right now?'

Immediately Jane began nodding her head vigorously. All she needed was the gag removed to allow her to speak about the coming stampede. Bannock hesitated, his manner suggesting he was sorry he could not indulge his sadism – then as he stooped to unfasten the kerchief knot at the back of the girl's head he hesitated and looked around him sharply.

'You hear somethin'?' he demanded of his men, as they too became attentive.

Jane shifted position agitatedly and again nodded her head, but the outlaw was too busy listening to notice her. He seemed to have forgotten about the gold. He was just able to catch the unmistakable lowing of cattle in the distance and a growling rumble, which, starting as a mere whispering echo, was gradually growing in power.

'Sweet hell, I get it!' one of the gunmen cried suddenly. 'It's a stampede, boss! Comin' from ways up the end of the canyon. Homburg and the dude must have started it: that's why we ain't seen 'em! If we're stuck here in front of a herd we don't stand a cat in hell's chance!'

Bannock was still not entirely convinced as he peered into the remote darkness at the far end of the narrow canyon. Then as the noise of the cattle and the thunder of their feet took on sudden loudness, as they came within the head of the canyon proper and the noise was imprisoned between the mighty walls, he jumped to his feet.

'You're right!' he gasped. *'Outa here – quick!'* And he dived for his horse.

'What about the dame?' one of the men shouted.

'To hell with her! She was probably in on this. She can have some of her own medicine – we'll find that gold by some other way!'

With no other thought in his head than to escape, Bannock leapt to the saddle and drove his spurs savagely into the animal's flanks. Too savagely, in fact. It shied wildly and lashed out its back feet, exploding the camp-fire into a deluge of sparks, burning wood, and flying stones.

Then the animal bolted forward, the roar of the stampeding herd not 200 yards to the rear. The three remaining men charged after the outlaw and caught up with him in a matter of seconds.

'Which way?' Sam yelled.

'The mesa!' Bannock shouted back. 'We can take a short cut over the mountain range and hit the desert. Only way to escape this herd...'

He swung his horse's head to one side and darted from the floor of the narrow canyon to the steeply shelving rock wall. In a moment or two he was amidst the low-growing trees and vegetation with which the rocks were clothed. He rode on doggedly, flogging the sweating animal over every obstacle, his three cohorts behind him engaged in a similar bitter struggle.

At least they had escaped the stampede. Though they could not actually see it for intervening vegetation, they could hear the din of the pounding hoofs and hear the moaning and blatting of the panic-stricken beasts.

'Hell's bells!' Bannock exclaimed suddenly, dragging to a halt. 'Take a look!'

His men caught up with him and gazed fixedly at their course ahead. It was blotted out by sweeping flame becoming ever fiercer, leaping from bush to bush and tree to tree, cloaking the valley side in an inferno.

'The camp-fire!' Bannock gasped. 'It got scattered, and it's set fire to the dry bushes in the canyon floor! The mesa's out: we can't make it through that. We'd better get back quick before we're cut off below, too. Just a chance the herd will have passed by now.'

He twirled his agitated horse round and started off down the perilous route up which he had come. Every yard's progress he made, slipping and sliding dangerously, he was only one jump ahead of the flames, the fire seizing on to every bush and thicket with devouring speed until, by now, the whole canyon side was illuminated by its flickering glare.

Reaching the far end of the valley floor again Bannock glanced back, his men just behind him. Every scrap of vegetation throughout the length of the valley floor was blazing, blotting out its more distant reaches in a curtain of flame. Of the stampeding cattle there was now no sign. Presumably, driven on by the fire, they had debouched on to the pastureland.

'Keep goin',' Bannock panted, as his men rode hard beside him. 'If we run into them cattle again we'll have room to turn around – which was more than we had in the canyon. By God, I'm goin' to git that dirty dude and Homburg for this night's work!'

'We can't just ride around,' Sam objected. 'I figure we oughta go into town and take over again. Once we git there we can work out our next move.'

'OK!' He gave a nod and flogged his tired mount on at a harder pace, drawing ever further away from the blaze in the canyon and pursuing the narrow arroyo, which led down through foothills to the open pastureland.

It was when they had reached it that they caught sight of the stampeded herd again. It was far to their right, a blackly moving mass under the stars.

'That makes us safe,' Bannock said in relief, slowing down a little. 'Them steers had me worried for a minute. Good thing in some ways that the fire stopped us vamoosing to the mesa, else we'd have had to keep goin'. As it is we're stoppin' – and we'll find that blasted gold, or else.'

His men said nothing. As far as they could see the chance of finding gold was further off than ever and, deep down, they were more than heartily sick of fighting the wholesale, ruthless methods of Meredith who, they had not the least doubt, had engineered this whole night's work.

And as the outlaws fled onwards towards the town they intended controlling once again, Meredith and his son were at the head of Rocky Canyon, watching the flames sweeping across its narrow vista and leap high to the mountain walls. With them were the ranchers and outfits from the Leaning-J and Bar-25.

'I don't like this at all, Dad,' Bart said worriedly, studying the holocaust. 'This fire's messed up everything! It's halted some of the steers, and others have gone from the valley floor to the canyon side to escape the flames. Taking it all round I very much doubt if Bannock and his boys have been overrun. This slow-up must have given them the chance to get away.'

'It weren't steers as started the fires, anyways,' one of the ranchers observed. 'It began afore they'd gotten halfway down the canyon. I reckon one of them outlaws knocked over his camp-fire or somethin' in his hurry to git out. Whatever the cause, it sure does look as though we ain't gettin' the straight run we'd figured on.'

'Well if it failed it can't be helped,' Meredith decided with his usual calm, sitting squarely on his stallion and surveying the proceedings. 'The unknown factor... But at least it would drive Bannock out of the valley much faster than he entered it.'

'Pretty cold comfort,' Bart growled.

'Don't worry, Son, we shall just have to devise other means of nailing him – perhaps even take the most sensible course, after all, and inform the authorities. In the meantime, our task is to recover these cattle before they get too spread out. I think the fire has abated sufficiently along the canyon floor. . . We'd better see.'

He nudged his stallion forward and it lumbered quickly through the midst of the rocks and presently into the canyon itself. The fire was now sweeping up the sides of the cleft, the trees and bushes brief torches, which cast off sparks to ignite other trees and bushes close at hand.

Meredith in the lead, the others followed, passing safely enough through the now extinguished regions until they gained the pastureland where in the distance they could now see the outline of the swarming cattle.

Meredith dragged his stallion to a halt and watched keenly, Bart and the ranchers catching up with him.

'It's goin' to be some job to round those up,' one of the ranchers remarked anxiously. 'Looks to me like they're still scared by the fire.'

'There's a greater problem,' Meredith remarked. 'It seems to me that the cattle are actually heading towards the town – and once they reach it, in their maddened state, that crazy structure is liable to be smashed to matchwood. At this hour nobody will be prepared for it; most of them sleeping. I think we should go into town and warn them!'

'You're right, Dad,' Bart agreed promptly. 'Let's go!'

He spurred his horse fiercely and Meredith beside him did likewise. Riding hard and taking a wide detour to avoid and get ahead of the cattle they covered the distance to Mountain Peak in record time, entering it to find the main street deserted, all lights out and the huddle of buildings leprous white in the starlight.

'Not much time,' one of the ranchers said. 'I guess this is the best way to start getting' folks movin'...'

He galloped his horse ahead of the others and, drawing his gun, fired it repeatedly into the air. After a moment or two windows opened and dim faces peered out into the night.

'*Stampede headed this way!*' the rancher yelled. 'Better get out! The buildings are likely to come down! *Step on it, all of you!* There ain't much time.'

He repeated his warning further up the street and, grasping the idea, the other rancher and the men from the two outfits did likewise. Bart and his father remained where they were, keeping a watch on the star-lit plateau for the first sign of the advancing herd ... until a grim voice made them turn sharply.

'Git off those cayuses, you lousy polecats! This is just what I've been waitin' for. Keep your hands up. And make it quick!'

'Bannock!' Bart exclaimed, staring at the dim figure only a yard away.

'Right,' the outlaw sneered. 'Mighty nice of you both to walk into town and warn us. And hurry it up, blast you!'

Further up the street the ranchers and their men were unaware of what had happened. One of the ranchers shouted, 'Come on, Bart, let's get outa here! We've done our part. If we don't quit we're liable to be trampled–What the hell you doin' back there?'

Bart dismounted and stood watching the ranchers and their men speed away into the distance. From the various buildings down the high street men and women came tumbling out and began heading in the same direction, away from the threatening danger.

Meredith also alighted with a thud and kept his hands raised. Bannock's gun glinted. Behind him there were now visible his three colleagues, waiting tensely.

'Well, dude, I reckon your effort to git rid of me and my boys didn't work, did it?' Bannock asked sourly.

'Never mind that,' Bart retorted. 'That stampede is headed this way. Once it gets here the lot of us are liable to be wiped out!'

'I'll be on my way with my boys by then,' the outlaw said. 'But you won't! Nor will this fat pig you tag along with. The stampede ain't gotten here yet,' he added. 'We'll hear it fast enough when it does and have enough warnin' to get clear. Right now I just want to tell you that I don't feel too sore about your attempt to kill us with that stampede in the canyon.'

'Nice of you – but I'm not particularly concerned, Bannock, how you feel!'

'No? You may be when I tell you why I ain't sore...' Bannock paused, enjoying the moment. 'It's because that stampede killed your wife!'

'*It – what?*' Bart gasped.

'Your wife– And keep those damned mitts of yours up! She was bound and gagged in the track of that stampede and couldn't have gotten away. I'd taken her from your ranch for two reasons: to find out where that gold is you've found, and to wipe her out in reprisal for Hank. Two can play at that game, feller!'

Bart breathed hard. He clenched his fists but did not dare lower his hands.

'If there was time I'd work you over until you told me about that gold – but there ain't. I can hear the first signs of the comin' stampede right now.' He turned sharply. 'OK, boys! Rope the jiggers up!'

The two men were quickly pinioned by wrists and ankles and the cords drawn tight. Finally Bannock performed his usual favourite trick and shoved them hard, overbalancing them into the dust of the street.

'Things are workin' out nicely,' he said. 'I gits rid of you and your wife all in one night and the town gits destroyed by cattle! The rest ought to be easy.'

He did not delay any longer. Taking Bart and his father's horses he joined his men and they darted away into the shadows. A few seconds later they were riding hell for leather for safety down the main street, trailing the stallion and mare behind them.

The town's inhabitants seemed to have gone too. The only sound on the night air was the distant lowing of cattle and the faint rumbling in the ground which denoted their advancing hoofs.

'Nothing could have saved Jane, Dad,' Bart panted, tearing hard and uselessly at his ropes. 'If she was bound up like us she couldn't have escaped the cattle – and even if she did that fire must have got her instead. By God, I've *got* to get free of this lot if only to settle accounts with that swine!'

'Do as I say, Son!' Meredith said urgently.

'There may be a way out of this! Brace your back against mine – that way we can get on our feet – hurry!'

Immediately Bart rolled over until his back was to his father's, then by dint of heaving and shoving they rocked up on their feet and remained balanced.

'Now hop, Son! Pogo-stick fashion – to the nearest window, smash the glass, and use it to cut these ropes. Come on!'

Meredith began jumping, cutting a remarkable figure bouncing up and down in the air as he progressed towards the board-walk. He reached it, Bart hopping after him. He was grimly conscious of the increased noise from the approaching herds. In a few minutes they would have reached town, and there being no other clear trail would be bound to sweep through it.

Reaching the window of the general store, its door swinging wide following the hurried departure of the inmates, Meredith rolled himself on to his back, then using his feet he drove them through the window glass. The pieces splintered into the store and on the boardwalk. He began wriggling swiftly towards a javelin-like barb only an inch or two away.

'Lie down, Son,' he instructed. 'Near to

me. I'll free you first.'

Bart threw himself flat, his back to his father. Meredith took a firm grip on the glass shard, then he sawed with it steadily until Bart felt his wrist-cords give way. The rest was simple. In the space of a few seconds he had himself free, and to release his father was only a moment's work. They both stood up listening to the din of the advancing herd.

'We can't outdistance these steers without our horses, and these buildings are too flimsy to give much protection,' Meredith panted.

It was a moment when swift thinking was necessary, but the only thing Bart could think of was the fate of Jane. He did not much care at the moment whether he himself lived or died.

'Have you the keys to the sheriff's office, Son?' Meredith asked abruptly.

'Eh?' Bart stirred out of his morbid reverie. 'Yes, sure I have. But what–?'

'I think we can save ourselves,' his father said. 'Quickly, Son – the sheriff's office.'

Bart followed Meredith's huge bulk along the boardwalk until they came to the sheriff's office – then his father motioned.

'Open it up – quickly!'

Bart wasted no time in doing so. 'I don't get this, Dad,' he said, puzzled. 'We didn't need to unlock the door. We could have have blasted the lock with our guns and–'

'Why waste bullets? But I require the keys for another purpose – namely the steel filing cabinets which no bullets would be able to break open.'

'Steel...?' Bart looked at him in mystification in the gloom – then with a shrug he led the way into the office's dark interior. The noise of the approaching stampede, little more than quarter of a mile away, was abruptly cut off.

'Here's the idea,' Meredith said, as they stopped in the centre of the small office. 'We have here two six-foot high steel cabinets full of records. If we each get into one of the cabinets – tipping the records out – and hold the door to from the inside we may survive if the building should fall down upon us. Iron-clad protection!'

Realizing the ingenuity of the idea, Bart wasted no time in unlocking the doors of the cabinets and lending a hand to whip out the records, and then tearing the shelves free of their grooves and tossing them on the floor. The job had only just been completed and both men had eased themselves into the cabinets' interiors – Meredith with a good deal of puffing because of his enormous bulk – when the shattering din of the stampede burst upon them. They both withdrew into their fortresses, the doors very slightly open so they could have some idea of what was transpiring.

The noise of the thundering herd was ground-shaking, and the first thing to go was the big office window. The din was immediately increased, made up of moaning cattle, the thud of bone against flesh, the crack and concussion of building supports giving way–

Then with a sudden impact the front of the office stove in under the pressure of the surging beasts' bodies. The floor sagged at the same moment and the two men both found themselves lying full length in their containers, deafened for a moment by the clangour of falling beams striking the cabinets in which they lay. They could no longer observe anything outside. The faint light was entirely blotted out by choking clouds of dust.

Then slowly, the chaos began to subside and the noise of the frightened beasts diminished with distance. Bart stirred and shoved the door of the filing cabinet, tipping away a mass of broken wood chippings and white powdery dust. He looked about him in the starlight. The roof had vanished and three of the walls had caved in, the fourth hanging over dangerously.

There was a sudden creaking and sound of breaking wood – then Meredith's head and shoulders emerged above the debris.

At a less critical moment Bart would have regarded the situation as comical. His father's face was smothered in white dust so that he looked like a miller who had too closely investigated a flour sack. Instead the death of his wife was in the forefront of his bitter thoughts.

'We've survived the stampede, but Jane has been killed because of it! It's horrible – I can't get over it, Dad.'

Meredith's voice was quiet as he answered. 'In the stress of the moment, Son, the matter had escaped me. But I cannot believe that Jane has come to any real harm. I just can't feel it somehow ... it wouldn't be *right*.'

Bart dragged himself free of the litter and stepped into the chaos of the main street. His father followed him and for a moment they stood gazing around them on the stricken buildings, most of them lopsided from the onslaught, and churned-up street and splintered boardwalks.

'At least Bannock now has nothing left to control.'

'To hell with Bannock!' Bart retorted. 'It's Jane I'm thinking about. We've got to look for her. If she's still alive – and I pray God that she is – she needs protection. And if she is ... dead, then she must have a decent funeral. Either way I must know what happened. Let's get going. Without our horses it's a long way to the canyon.'

And without giving his father time to respond Bart strode away determinedly.

# 7

## WITHIN THE CAVE

Jane was not dead. At the moment when Bannock leapt for his horse she was more or less certain that the oncoming cattle, still at the head of the canyon, would overwhelm her and trample her in the dust.

Then, in kicking wildly at the vicious stab of the spurs, the outlaw's mount smashed the camp-fire stonework to pieces and hurled the blazing fragments in all directions. Some of them narrowly missed Jane as she lay struggling on the ground; then she watched in alarm as nearby bushes, dry as tinder from the incessant blaze of the sun, flared abruptly and hurled their sparks to the next nearest vegetation – until within the space of a few seconds she was surrounded by a blazing ring of fire, yet untouched herself by reason of the arid sand on which she lay.

Transfixed, she watched the surging fire as the night wind fanned it, listening to the crackle of the burning vegetation and, further away, the thunder of the steers' hoofs. Then she began to glimpse them, first in two and threes, then in dozens, as they surged past beyond the outer perimeter of the fire-ring, some of them stumbling amidst the rocks, panic-stricken, moaning, shoving against each other, doing all in their power to avoid the flames flashing towards them.

A chunk of smouldering branch, blown by the disturbed air-currents, rolled in Jane's direction. She wriggled quickly from it, watched it come to a stop, and then making up her mind she edged forward again and put her ankle ropes across it, straining her feet apart as she did so. Her boots protected her somewhat from heat as, after a moment or two the rope began to smoulder – then the strain she threw on it snapped it.

Her wrists were a more difficult matter and she burned herself excruciatingly in the process, but at the price of blisters and smarting flesh she finally singed the cords through and released her hands.

Standing up, she tugged the gag from her mouth and looked about her. In all directions except one the fire surrounded her. The one route that had not yet been closed lay up the mountainside, and even this course was obviously threatened if she did not move fast. To stay here as the fire burned away from her in an ever-widening circle was to risk that the cattle – still advancing – might plunge in upon her – or else she could try and climb the mountainside.

Hesitating only a moment, she raced quickly along the narrow, flame-bordered vista, dodged the hurtling bodies of two steers, and then began to scramble up the rocks of the mountain face. She had hardly started on the rough, difficult ascent before the flames closed below and behind her and began to follow relentlessly.

Breathing hard, dishevelled, her clothes torn with the rough stones, she continued the ascent, glancing back now and again beyond the flames to the surging cattle visible around the outermost edges of the fire.

So, gradually, she climbed to the regions where the vegetation clung but sparsely and the danger from fire was gone. Breathing hard, she settled amidst the rocks, considered her blistered wrists, and then tore half the sleeves from her blouse and wrapped the fabric round the burns, throwing away the loose pieces. This done she looked below. The fire was still spreading along the canyon floor from its circular core and the cattle, if they were present, were masked by smoke and gloom. Only the noise of them still rose to the heights.

Jane judged that it would be some time before the fire burned itself out sufficiently below to allow her to descend. In the meantime the night air was cold, the frigid wind blowing down the mountain face from the cloudless sky. She shivered in her thin blouse, now even less of a protection with most of the sleeves ripped away.

To remain sitting here was asking for pneumonia – and to ascend any higher would only make things colder. To go below until more of the vegetation had burned itself to ash was impossible – so she got up wearily and looked about her.

She had assumed that the cliff face opposite her was solid, but a closer inspection as she moved along beside it proved her wrong. There was a small natural cave opening a hundred yards away from her along the ill-defined acclivity she was following.

With a thankful sigh she hurried towards it, grateful for the slight warmth it held as she entered it. Here she was protected from the biting night wind and some of the heat of the day still lingered in the cave's recesses.

Settling down on its floor she rested for a while, watching the spread of flames some 200 feet below. She could see no more than this; then curiosity got the better of her. Rising, she began to explore her haven, feeling her way along the rocky wall, surprised to discover that the cave was more of a tunnel than anything else, going straight into the main bulk of the range.

She had no light, but the fascination of exploring was upon her so she crept on slowly, feeling every inch of the way in case she fell into an unexpected crevice or internal chasm. The floor remained solid, however, and after a while the sense of emptiness about her and the echo of her footfalls amidst the loose stone of the tunnel floor told her she had entered some kind of cavern. She came to a halt and stood staring blindly into the dark.

Nowhere was there a spark of light, the cavern lying well within the range. Satisfied, and not daring to go any further, she put out her hand to find the rock wall again – and instead contacted something rough and splintery. She added her other hand to the investigation and finally arrived at the conclusion that there were a number of wooden boxes stored here – and they had evidently been standing some time for upon the top-most she could distinctly feel a thick layer of soft dust.

Never had she wished more desperately for a light than at this moment. Quite possibly here was the very Wells-Fargo cargo which Bannock and his men were looking for! She only needed a glimmer, however brief, to satisfy her suspicion. She thought for a moment and then hit on the only possibility. Two stones struck together might provide sparks by which she might be able to see something.

Excitement overcame caution. She went on her knees and began a hurried search of the floor for loose stones, but apparently there were few to be found. Then suddenly, as she moved around, she became aware of the cavern floor vibrating beneath her. She got up quickly, but not quickly enough. The floor gave way under her weight and she felt herself hurtling downwards in the inky blackness to strike rock with numbing impact. A violent pain shot the length of her right leg and remained. She lay breathing hard in the dark, her teeth clenched.

There were no sounds save the tumbling of a few odd stones from above. She moved, or at least attempted to do so, then the pain in her leg forced her to relax again. She did not need any imagination to realize that she had almost certainly broken it.

It was not long before Meredith caught up with Bart as he strode determinedly across the grassland in the direction of the mountain range. Wheezing somewhat from his exertions his father fell into step.

'You realize that you have embarked on a ten-mile walk,' he remarked. 'A trifle to you, perhaps – but not to me!'

'If you can think of any other way of getting to Rocky Canyon to try and find Jane when we haven't got horses, let's hear it,' Bart said, anxiety sharpening his voice.

'I was going to suggest that we bear to our right where – unless my eyes are playing me tricks – I believe I can see the ranchers and their men rounding up the cattle...'

Meredith broke off as shots exploded into the air in the distance followed by bellowing cries.

'Ah, I was right,' he added. 'We might borrow a couple of horses from them...'

Bart shook his head. 'It would take us as long to reach them and get the horses as it would to get half way to the Canyon – and every moment counts. We'll go on walking.'

Meredith sighed, and tramped on steadily with the silent Bart at his side.

To Meredith at least it seemed an age before they left the grassland behind and came to sandy regions, which marked the commencement of the arroyo that led in a twisted, moonlit trail into Rocky Canyon.

Untiring, anxiety driving him on, Bart strode through the sand and grass-tufts – until a grim voice suddenly halted him in his tracks.

'Take it easy, you two! You're covered!'

'Bannock, I fancy,' Meredith commented grimly, raising his hands and waiting.

He was right. In a second or two, the outlaw and his three cohorts came riding into view from behind a nearby outcropping of trees. Whilst his men kept their guns levelled, Bannock slid from the saddle and came over, taking the two men's guns from them and stuffing them in his own belt.

'Nice coincidence, I reckon,' he said grimly, his face hardly visible in the moonlight under the shadow of his sombrero. 'We happened to see you as we was ridin' back from Rocky Canyon. It seems like I've got me a job to do all over again. Looks like you side-tracked that stampede...'

'Very observant of you,' Meredith said

drily; then he staggered and fell on hands and knees in the sand as the flat of the outlaw's hand struck him viciously across the face.

'You can shut your mouth, Homburg! I'm gettin' kinda sick of your cracks. Not that you'll be in fit shape to make many more of 'em anyways. This strikes me as a heaven-sent opportunity to finish things here instead of with the stampede.'

'How about my wife?' Bart demanded. 'You say you've come back from Rocky Canyon. Was she there?'

'Course not!' Bannock laughed shortly. 'You didn't expect her to be, did you? She'd be crushed and carried along with the herd – her body might be just any place. Too bad, ain't it?'

'So help me, Bannock, I'll get you for this night's work!'

'Stop talkin' like a fool! There ain't nothin' you can do now or at any time – and anyway, it was *your* idea to start the stampede, not mine!'

'It was your idea to kidnap my wife and then leave her when the cattle started moving!'

'What else do you expect from a sadistic moron like Bannock, Son?' Meredith said, and the outlaw's head jerked.

'I thought I warned you, Homburg, against makin' cracks! Any more like that and I'll break your legs!'

'You're welcome to try,' Meredith replied evenly, his hands still raised.

There was a moment's pause, then stung by the cynicism in Meredith's voice the outlaw came forward with his gun pointed. Meredith remained motionless, Bart narrowly watching him and wondering vaguely if he had some kind of scheme in mind. He had – and as usual it was devastatingly simple.

When the outlaw had come within two feet of him Meredith threw both his raised hands forward abruptly and into the outlaw's face he rained a stinging dust of fine sand from two directions at once. Bannock spluttered, the grit momentarily blinding him – then the vast stomach hit him in the midriff and he toppled over on his back.

'Down!' Meredith snapped, flinging himself forward as he spoke, and Bart thudded beside him, just in time to miss the bullets from the nearby watching gunmen.

Missing the first time, they lost their advantage. Meredith seized Bannock firmly and used him as a shield in front of himself

184

and Bart, digging his retrieved gun relentlessly into the outlaw's spine. Reaching forward, Bart took the outlaw's gun into his own fingers.

'Do you still feel that you would like to break my legs?' Meredith murmured.

'Yeah, blast you – and I will yet! What do you reckon you can do with my men coverin' you?'

'I think you'd better tell them to toss their guns over here. If they don't, a bullet will find its way into your heart – through your back!'

'Get busy telling 'em – or die!' Bart snapped. 'I'm happy either way!'

'OK, boys,' Bannock growled. 'Do as he says. He's got the drop on us – for now.'

The three outlaws tossed across their guns and, using his great weight, Meredith ground them with his heel right down into the sand, making them unusable without very meticulous cleaning.

'Well, now what?' Bannock snapped. 'Goin' to shoot me in the back. I suppose?'

'That technique is more appropriate to you than either of us,' Meredith said. 'However, I do intend to repay you with interest for the blow you delivered a moment ago.'

'There's no time for monkeying around,

185

Dad!' Bart objected. 'We must find out what's happened to Jane first, and then–'

'These rats must be incapacitated before that can be done,' Meredith reminded him. 'Hold my gun and keep these other scum covered whilst I deal with Bannock.'

Bart took the gun somewhat ill-humouredly and levelled it opposite the one in his right hand. Meredith dragged the outlaw on to his feet, spinning him round to face him.

'Now,' he said calmly, 'I invite you to try and break my legs!'

Bannock hesitated, convinced that there ought not to be much difficulty in handling this obese fool in the Homburg hat, and yet somehow sensing that Meredith had some trick to play.

Finally the outlaw plunged, diving straight for Meredith's legs. The tackle was never completed for suddenly Meredith slammed up his right boot. It struck the outlaw a fiendish crack under the jaw and snapped his teeth together, just missing guillotining his tongue. His head singing as though it would explode he found himself on hands and knees with Meredith now to one side of him instead of in the front.

Regardless of his pain, Bannock whirled

on to his feet and charged straight at the waiting Meredith. He remained immovable until the last second, then, bracing his legs, he thrust out his colossal equator and withstood the shock of Bannock cannoning into it.

The outlaw actually seemed to Bart to rebound a slight distance and before he could recover himself Meredith's right whirled up and the bunched knuckles smote Bannock under his already agonized jaw. Lights burst in front of him, increasing to bewildering brilliance as another blow descending downwards struck him violently across the bridge of the nose.

Meredith's final move was simple enough. He brought up his right leg in a scything movement round the back of the outlaw's knees as he staggered giddily. Promptly his legs folded and he sat down with a thump, blood trickling from his nose and his mouth opening and shutting.

'As you remarked, time is pressing,' Meredith commented, turning to Bart. 'If we bind him – and his men – to that outcropping of trees there, I think we shall find them again when we have finished looking for Jane: then we can hand them over or do whatever else we may decide is necessary.'

'Shoot 'em and be done with it,' Bart growled. 'They killed Jane, didn't they?'

'Not directly, son – nor are we sure she's dead. Shooting is really too good for any of these men. If we delay our return they will suffer quite a deal once the day comes, especially with no water handy... There should be some ropes on the horses there – cover me whilst I have a look.'

Bart nodded grimly and kept his guns ready, but the three standing outlaws knew better than to defy them in the mood Bart was in; and Bannock for his part was too knocked about and pain-racked to raise resistance anyway.

With his men he was bound to the nearest of the trees, and Meredith, who knew practically every knot there was to know, made a secure job of the ropes. Then he stood back and considered his handiwork in the moon-light.

'We will return when we can,' he said, raising his Homburg mockingly. 'In the meantime, I trust you will enjoy sun-bathing here when the day comes.'

Sullen-faced in the dim light, none of them said anything. Meredith motioned and with Bart made for the horses. Swiftly they mounted their own stallion and mare, then, trailing the outlaws' mounts beside them, they headed at a quick gallop along the sandy arroyo. As they rode, Meredith took back the gun he had given into Bart's charge.

'I still think we'd have done better to have shot the swine,' Bart said bitterly, as he looked about him in the moonlight. 'If they get free it will mean we've lost our chance of blotting them out.'

'Strangely enough, I cannot bring myself to doing it when face to face with a defenceless man.'

'You did it to Hank,' Bart pointed out.

'With Hank it was different. For one thing he had a gun in his hand; for another my aim might have been bad – and further, one of the gang had to die in reprisal for a murder which we knew had been committed – namely, Milburn. Here we have no murder to avenge, not even Jane's since we don't know as yet what has happened to her. And in any case the stampede, directly responsible for whatever her plight may be, was not Bannock's doing.'

'Never mind whitewashing him!' Bart snapped. 'I still think we should have shot him point blank.'

'There was nothing to prevent you doing

so, Son, yet you refrained.'

'All right, Dad, you win!' Bart sighed. 'I can't shoot at a man point blank, either – not even a skunk like Bannock.'

The topic was dropped and before long the journey up the arroyo was finished and the mighty fissure of Rocky Canyon loomed ahead, quiet now the cattle had passed, but the moonlight revealed the churned-up earth where the hoofs had pounded. There was, too, a stirring of grey ash as the remains of the fire blew on the night wind.

'I can't understand how Jane seems to have disappeared,' Bart said, nudging the mare along slowly. 'Do you believe she was carried along by the herd?'

'Unlikely,' Meredith replied, after some thought. 'The best thing we can do is find out exactly what course the herd took from their hoofprints and then try to determine how – or if – Jane became involved.'

He dropped from the saddle and Bart did likewise. Tethering their own and the outlaws' horses to a blackened stump they began to advance on foot, studying the ground as they went. After a while Meredith came to a stop and pointed.

'Observe, Bart! Two divergent cattle trails coming from either side of the canyon and forming into one – leaving the centre clear. We know that Bannock had his camp in the centre, so with a little luck we might even find the marks of where he had his camp-fire.'

He hurried ahead with Bart right beside him. Around the middle of the valley floor there were no cattle trails at all. To distinguish where the campfire had been was now impossible owing to the many blackened areas from the brush fire. Meredith stood looking about him and contemplating the mighty walls of the canyon. Finally he pointed.

'That is the approximate position where we were – so Bannock must have had his camp about this spot. Since the area is clear of hoofs around here I think we may assume that Jane was not involved in the stampede. Naturally Bannock would bring her to his camp.'

'Then – where is she?'

Bart looked about him for a while; then he cupped his hands and shouted her name several times. The echoes gave it back to him, and that was all.

'She had two choices,' his father commented, musing. 'She could go right or left and either way would– No!' He broke off, shaking his head. 'To the left *only*. There are

signs that on the right a good deal of vegetation must have been aflame, but to the left
the vegetation is sparser. I think we had
better look that way.'

Bart nodded, falling into step beside his
father. They looked intently at the ground as
they moved; then Meredith halted abruptly
and went down on one knee. In the moonlight he studied the baked earth.

'Look – the imprint of a small high-heel,
identical I would say to Jane's riding boots...
And beyond here the churned-up earth
caused by the passage of cattle. Fortunately
the earth is not so hard that it will not take
a narrow high-heel imprint. It would seem
that Jane did come this way...'

'And got herself involved in the cattle
sweeping past!' Bart declared bleakly.

'Not necessarily. We have no means of
knowing whether she passed this way before
or after the cattle. If she was involved in
their midst her prints will cease at the point
beyond the track they have made. If not...
Well, we may still be able to trail her. Definitely she came this way.'

Meredith got up clumsily and went ahead,
his gaze fixed on the ground. Bart kept
beside him, hardly daring to hope that the
prints might continue beyond the trail of the

cattle. Upon this one factor depended the answer as to whether or not Jane had been swept away by the herd.

'Here they are, Bart!' Meredith cried, a little way ahead. 'Continuing!'

Bart rushed up to him and found him beaming in the moonlight as he pointed to the ground. The sandy, baked floor of the valley was just commencing to give place at this point to a harder rock of the mountain-side proper, but there was no denying the heel prints Jane had left behind in her hurried climb to the upper regions.

'Then she's alive, Dad!' Bart cried thank-fully. 'At least we know that much!'

'Our problem now is to discover where she has gone. It's possible that she may have returned home once the cattle had passed – though I don't think she would do that without trying to contact us first. She would probably be too frightened to return after the way Bannock managed to capture her.'

'Which reminds me,' Bart said grimly. 'When we get back to the spread I'll blast those boys of ours wide open for letting it happen. Anyway, let's carry on.'

He megaphoned his hands and bawled 'Jane!' with all his power several times – but there was no answering cry. He shrugged and looked at the frowning rock climbing into the star and moonlit sky.

'She must have gone up this narrow acclivity,' Meredith said, indicating it, 'to escape the fire which seems to have swept up here in its travels. Let us see what we can find.'

Securely tied to the tree where Meredith and Bart had left them, Bannock and his three comrades struggled savagely for a while to free themselves – and then gave it up.

Bannock in particular, worn out after his battle with Meredith, had not the energy to struggle much at first. But after a while his strength began to return and with it a surging fury.

'What in hell are we standin' here like blasted dummies for?' he demanded. 'Whilst we're here those two skunks could be diggin' out that gold! They headed for the canyon.'

'Yeah, but only to try and find the dame,' Sam growled.

'If we could only git the drop on 'em whilst they're in the canyon, we could make 'em talk about where the gold is.' Bannock began to struggle savagely.

'How are we goin' to do that?' one of the men asked morosely. 'That pot-bellied old buzzard sure knows how to make knots that stick!'

'There might be one way,' Bannock said, after thinking. 'I've a jack-knife they missed – in my hip pocket, but I don't think I can get at it. You have a try, Baldy: you're right next to me an' your left hand might just reach it if you strain a bit this way.'

Baldy's hands, like those of the others, were knotted securely behind his back, his entire body roped to the tree with the other men in a similar position. But by straining his body forward a fraction of an inch he could at least drag his hand a little to one side.

By jerks he succeeded in moving them until, by Bannock thrusting his hip to the right and Baldy straining to the left, they came within touching distance.

'Anywhere near it?' Bannock demanded, panting.

'Yeah – yeah, I think I can make it.'

Baldy edged his fingers forward and finally got a grip on the top of Bannock's hip-pocket. There was another pause, then with the cords cutting savagely into his skin he wriggled his fingers into the recess, got the knife between his first and second fingers and dragged it out.

'Got it!' he breathed. 'Now to get it open...'

He made several efforts before he succeeded; then he turned the sharp edge of the blade towards himself and began a sawing movement between his wrists. Because of the lack of pressure it took him some time to slice the cord, but at last it gave way and his wrists were suddenly free. To release the others was but the work of a few moments. Bannock took the knife back from him and gazed about.

'OK, that's that,' he said, setting his mouth. 'Now we'll head for Rocky Canyon, where there's a good chance we'll find Dude and Homburg. Then I'll find out about the gold from 'em first and kill 'em second. I reckon they're both a damned sight too dangerous to live.'

'Far as I'm concerned I ain't feelin' in the mood for walkin' to that damned canyon,' Sam objected. 'It must be ten miles away!'

'You'll walk and like it, feller,' Bannock sneered. 'Those jiggers have taken our cayuses. But before we do we'd best try and find them guns they threw away.'

But though they searched very carefully for nearly fifteen minutes in the bright moonlight they were unlucky. The guns had vanished when Meredith had stamped them into the sand, and there was little hope of finding them.

'Hell, Jack, we'll need our hardware to deal with those two,' Baldy complained.

'While it remains dark we can git away with it,' Bannock said obstinately. 'If we run into 'em they won't know if we've got guns or not. We can bluff 'em and git their guns. We're riskin' it, anyways – and we're wastin' time. Come on!'

He began to move with dogged resolve through the sandy waste. His men hesitated and looked at each other; then, because there was nothing else they could do, they began to follow him.

The silent quartet tramped through what remained of the sandy stretches and presently gained the pasture-lands. It was perfectly clear to his men that Bannock was intent on revenge – even more than learning about the gold. Nothing else would have driven him to such foot-slogging effort through such difficult country.

Hard though all the men were they found it tough going through seemingly endless grassy wastes, then across more desert outcroppings, then stony stretches, and finally sand again as they neared the foot of the arroyo leading to the canyon.

'Watch yourselves,' Bannock said curtly. 'I guess anythin' can happen. Keep on the grass near as you can – this sandy stuff will outline us in the moonlight.'

The men said nothing. They followed him wearily, quite convinced by this time that there ought to be easier ways of tracing a stolen gold consignment.

# 8

## MEREDITH'S MASTER-STROKE

Meredith came to a halt in the moonlight and stooped. He picked up some fragments of green fabric and studied them, Bart looking over his shoulder.

'That's the same colour as one of Jane's blouses!' Bart exclaimed excitedly.

'It looks as if she came this way all right,' Meredith agreed, 'and either accidentally or deliberately tore away part of her blouse in the doing.' He thought for a moment, then: 'Since there aren't any jagged projections here, it may have been deliberately torn. Perhaps she needed a bandage of some kind...'

'Which means she's hurt,' Bart muttered. 'She may even be unconscious, which is why she doesn't answer...' He peered about him in the gloom. 'There seems to be only one way we can go from here: straight up this slope.'

'Yes, and there's a cave opening up there. See it? No guarantee that Jane went into it, but it's a possibility.'

The two men started forward again and in a few moments had entered the cave.

'Jane!' Bart called sharply into the dark. 'Jane, are you around here anywhere?'

There was no response. He was trying to think what next to do when his father stuck a match and held its weak yellow flame over his head.

'It's not a cave, Bart – it's a tunnel!' he said.

'Surely Jane would have no reason to go along back there?'

'I suppose not... We might try one more call, anyway.'

'*Jane!*' Bart yelled, megaphoning his hands. 'Jane! Are you there?'

'Here!' came a reply, so faint and distant it might have been on another planet.

'Dad! Did you hear something, or was it a – a sort of echo?'

'I think it was Jane's voice! Somewhere in the tunnel ahead...'

Without hesitating any further, Meredith hurried along it and another match scraped into life and flared as he went, its light flickering against rough walls. It expired just as he reached the point where the tunnel branched into the cave.

Pausing he struck a fresh one and looked about him.

'Just look at that!'

Bart nodded to four cases stacked against the wall, one on top of the other, then he gave a little gasp as he saw faded stencilled words WELLS-FARGO on each one.

'Apparently we've found it,' Meredith observed, unmoved. 'However, finding Jane is the priority. Perhaps she is over there,' he added, nodding to a collapsed portion of the cavern floor, and he hurried towards it quickly.

Lying beside it he peered into the depths. From below Jane had evidently seen the match flame and heard the conversation, for her voice came floating up.

'That you, Bart? Oh, thank heaven.'

'It's me, Jane – Randle. But Bart is here.'

'You bet I am!' Bart flung himself down quickly at his father's side. 'What's happened, Jane? How far down are you?'

'I don't exactly know, but I'd say about fifteen feet. I can't get up, Bart; my leg's broken or something.'

'It's what!' he exclaimed, concerned. 'Hold on; I'll be down with you in no time. Stand by to give me a hand up, Dad.'

'Certainly.'

Meredith struck another match and held the glimmering flame aloft as Bart felt his way over the crumbled cavity edge and then let himself fall. The drop was greater than he had imagined. Just before the match glimmer expired he had time to see Jane beside him. In another moment his arms were about her.

'Thank God you found me, Bart,' she whispered, and he could feel her quivering. 'I thought I was finished – lost down here in the dark with my leg broken. I couldn't possibly manage to climb back.'

'How on earth did you get into this hole, anyway?' Bart demanded.

'I – I fell in. The floor gave way. I was looking for two stones to strike on each other and make a light when it happened. You've seen those cases back there, I suppose? Are they Wells-Fargo stuff?'

'Yes.'

'I guessed as much, but having no light I couldn't be certain.'

There was a moment's pause then as Bart's fingers came in contact with the girl's wrists he spoke again. 'What's all this bandaging for? Is it part of your blouse torn up?'

'Uh-huh. I burned my wrists escaping from the canyon,' and the girl related what had happened.

'You leaving scraps of your blouse lying about guided us here,' Bart said. 'First thing to do is to get you above. Come on – drape yourself over my shoulder... That's it.'

She obeyed and he struggled up with her in position and looked above him.

'Ready, Son?' Meredith's voice enquired from the dark.

'Yes, if you can reach down this far. I've got Jane over my shoulder so there'll be considerable weight.'

'I've removed my pants' leather belt. If you can grasp it, I can try and pull you up. My only anxiety is that my trousers are deprived of support.'

'In the dark that shouldn't worry you,' Bart gave a dry chuckle. 'OK, Dad – get busy.'

There was the sound of the heavy belt-buckle clinking against the rock just overhead. Bart felt around until he could grasp it; then he threw his own and Jane's weight upon it.

'Go ahead, Bart,' Meredith called. 'I am well braced.'

Bart obeyed, using both hands, digging the toes of his boots into the roughness of the rocks to ease the strain, until he gradually managed to fight his way to the top. The moment he released his hold of the belt and clung to the rock instead, Meredith reached down and lifted Jane clear. After that the rest was easy.

'Many thanks,' Bart panted. 'I guess you can put your belt back on again.'

There was the sound of Meredith's movements, then another match flared in the blackness and Jane was visible stretched on the floor, her blouse with torn sleeves and she herself covered in dirt.

'Think you can do anything with the leg, Randle?' she asked, and both men saw her teeth clench in pain just before the light expired again.

'No reason why not,' Bart answered. 'Dad knows how to handle most things. But we need some decent light. How about some wood from those crates over there?'

'An excellent idea, Son. I'll see what I can do. If her leg is fractured we'll need splints as well.'

There was the sound of feet moving over to the crates, then Meredith struck a match to investigate them more closely. Finally, working in the dark again, he began operations with his jack-knife and after a while there was the teeth-edging squeak of wood parting from rusty nails.

He returned with six long slats, match flame glimmering, which he applied to one of the slats – unsuccessfully at first. After splitting it up with his knife into thinner sections he had enough to make a modest fire and, being dust-dry, the wood began to burn almost immediately.

Bart watched the gathering flame and nodded.

'Good enough! Keep it fed, Dad – I'll take a look what's wrong with Jane then you can do your stuff.'

It did not take him long to locate the fracture, between knee and ankle. With his father's help, both of them using their shirts for bandaging and two of the slats cut to length for splints they did what they could with makeshift first-aid.

'That should keep it OK until we can get you to the doc for proper treatment, Jane,' Bart said finally, smiling. 'You sure do seem to have taken it on the chin lately!'

'So did Bannock,' Meredith commented, putting more wood on the fire.

'What happened about him?' Jane asked, shifting into a sitting position with Bart's help. 'Did the stampede get him as you planned?'

'Unfortunately no...' Bart sighed, and then he added the details of the experiences through which he and his father had passed.

'Sounds like you've had an even tougher time than me,' Jane commented. 'Are you now going to contact the authorities in Wilson City and hand those outlaws over?'

'That's it. We should have taken the risk and done it long ago instead of trying to play the game our way.' Bart got on his feet. 'Anyway, whilst we're here we'd better find out what is in these cases, then we can tell the authorities about them too.'

'Apparently, an entire Wells-Fargo consignment,' Meredith said, going over to the cases in the flickering firelight. 'Four cases in all and presumably gold in each one. Certainly there is in this top one. Look for yourself.'

Bart did so, studying the yellow metal, all of it made up in ingots with an indented government stamp upon them.

'And worth a fortune,' he commented. 'If we were dishonest and kept quiet about this lot, we could live in the lap of luxury for the rest of our lives.'

'I've no wish to do that, Son. But in any case we will be entitled to collect the reward for this gold, and we can consider that fair compensation. So, we'll inform the authorities, and–'

'Yeah?' a voice asked laconically. 'That's what you think, Fatty! You're covered! Git your blasted hands up – and you too, dude! And don't turn around, neither.'

'Take it easy, Bart!' Jane called in alarm. 'They're right behind you.'

As Bart raised his hands he felt his gun taken from his belt, and his father too was deprived of his weapon. Then Bannock's voice spoke again.

'OK, you mugs – you can turn round now. Just as well you didn't do it sooner because I'd no gun!'

Furious as they realized the advantage they had lost, the two men turned slowly to behold Bannock in the flickering firelight, the two guns levelled, his three side-kicks immediately behind him, in the tunnel mouth.

'Surprised?' the outlaw asked. 'Mebbe you should learn to tie knots all over again, potbelly! We knew you'd be makin' for Rocky Canyon, so we followed you. When we saw the horses roped up down below – our own cayuses amongst 'em – the rest didn't take much guessin'.'

Bannock's eyes strayed across to Jane.

207

'What's the matter with the dame?' he asked briefly.

'Broken leg!' Bart snapped.

'Yeah? Pity it weren't her blasted neck. Mebbe it will be afore I'm finished.' Bannock's mouth set. 'I've got a drop on you, and I ain't forgotten the way you kicked me around, Homburg, neither!'

Neither Meredith nor Bart said anything. Out of the corner of his eye Bart could see that Jane was performing some kind of action, but he did not dare look directly because the outlaw would follow his gaze – so he did his best to hold Bannock's attention, with his father's assistance.

'I think, Son,' Meredith said gravely, 'that you were right in saying we should have shot these men when we had the chance. I now deeply regret my leniency.'

Bannock grinned crookedly. 'You'll more than regret it, feller, believe me..!'

He got no further. Jane, who had wriggled her way unnoticed to the gradually expiring fire, suddenly whipped up a half consumed piece of lath and hurled it across the cavern. It hit Bannock on the shoulder and he instantly reached towards it. Simultaneously Bart's fist crashed into his jaw and sent him flying backwards.

Bannock collided with the wall and fired savagely, missing. The bullet landed in the second crate from the bottom. Bart flung himself forward, low down, and the gun exploded again – but this time Bart was quick enough to knock the outlaw's gun-hand upwards so that the bullet snicked rock and brought small pieces pelting down. Then he closed with the outlaw, wrenched away the remaining gun, and rained blows at him.

Meredith was not idle either. Charging straight into the three remaining unarmed men, he sent one spinning and slammed the heads of the remaining two together with savage impact. Even Jane, some distance away, heard the collision of the two skulls and winced.

But Meredith's advantage was short-lived. In making a second plunge he caught his foot against an irregularity in the rock floor, stumbled, and then was knocked off-balance by a hammer blow from the nearest man. Before he could save himself he was on his back, a man kneeling on each arm and the third sitting astride his chest.

Bart, startled to find his father beaten for once, glanced at him in the dying light of the fire – and then went staggering backwards from a terrific crack on the jaw. He sat down and shook his head dazedly. When the blur had gone from his eyes he found himself looking at Bannock's gun muzzle as he stood over him.

'On your feet!' the outlaw commanded.

Bart obeyed slowly, realizing his advantage had gone. Jane put some more wood on the fire and the flickering brightness returned to the cavern. Meredith lay inert, looking intently at the four cases by the wall, and the round hole where Bannock's bullet had driven through the woodwork. Then he looked up again as the outlaw spoke.

'OK, boys, let Homburg get up.'

Meredith was released and heaved himself to his feet, pulling his Homburg back into place.

'All right, let's get on with the shooting,' Bart snapped.

Bannock grinned in the firelight. 'What's the matter, feller? Tired of life? I'll finish you off when I'm good and ready. First you're goin' to git some work done and save me and my boys doin' it. We're about bushed after trampin' half over the earth after you.'

'Work?' Meredith repeated, frowning.

'Yeah. I guess it'll take your blubber down a bit, Fatty. You see them cases there? Top one's got gold bricks in it, so the rest'll be the same. It'll be no easy job to carry 'em out and down to the horses, so I guess you two mugs can do it. There's four cayuses down there, and four crates. You can fasten a crate to each horse. When you've done that I'll dispose of you. Neat, huh?'

'You think we'd do that?' Bart demanded. 'Carry the gold for you before getting wiped out? Like hell!'

'Why not, Son?' Meredith asked, shrugging. 'There is an old saying – "Whilst there's life there's hope". We may even find a way to defeat these gunnies before they decide to finish us. Every second gained is useful.'

'You're livin' in a fool's paradise, Homburg,' Bannock told him. 'You'll soon be dead meat for the buzzards.' He laughed harshly. 'You'll keep 'em fed for weeks, I reckon! OK,' he motioned with his gun, 'get that top case on its way.'

Meredith hesitated and seemed to be thinking. Then, his face becoming moonishly innocent he seized hold of the topmost case and pulled it. It budged slightly, but that was all. Its weight was tremendous.

'Give him a hand,' Bannock snapped to Bart – and catching Meredith's look, he obeyed. By dint of considerable effort he

211

and his father got the case on opposite shoulders and carried it between them.

'Take it down to the horses,' the outlaw ordered. 'Here, Baldy, take this gun and see that they do it – And if you mugs try any funny business don't forgit that the dame's still here.'

The two men said nothing. Supporting the heavy weight between them they went along the tunnel in the darkness and into the grey light of the approaching dawn. Carrying the crate down the rough mountain trail was exhausting work: to secure it to the saddle of the strongest-looking of the four horses was even harder. But they finally managed it, attempting no tricks since Baldy's gun was trained on them and Jane's life was at stake if they made one false move.

The two men looked at each other – Bart anxious and tight-lipped; Meredith round-eyed and innocent as a baby ... then they returned up the slope and entered the cave.

'All right, now the next one,' Bannock directed. 'Still three left, so you've plenty to do. Hurry up and get movin'.'

Meredith dragged at it and with Bart's help settled it on the floor with a thump. This done he straightened and mopped his face.

'Findin' it tough?' Bannock asked drily. 'Do you good! You're too blasted fat anyways!'

'I fear you may be right,' Meredith sighed. 'Before proceeding further would you grant my son and I permission to have a smoke? Just one last cigarette each?'

'OK,' the outlaw assented, the request amusing him. 'But I'll get it and light it for you! I'm not chancin' any tricks!'

He fished in his shirt pocket and jerked a battered half-empty packet from it, pushing two of the weeds forward. Bart and his father both took one. Striking a match on the seat of his pants with his free hand, Bannock lighted the cigarettes, then one for himself.

'Enjoy it,' he invited, grinning. 'Be the last ones you'll ever have!'

Meredith inhaled gratefully and allowed smoke to trickle from his nostrils. Presently his eyes strayed to Jane, still half lying by the fire, keeping it fed.

'Might I enquire what you intend doing to Jane?' Meredith asked, looking at the outlaw.

'Shootin' her when I'm good and ready – same as with you mugs!'

Meredith smoked pensively for a moment or two then he said, 'I think that now is the time when we can perhaps make a bargain with you, Bannock.'

'*Bargain?*' the outlaw repeated, frowning. 'You loco, Homburg? I ain't makin' no blasted bargains! You'll clear this gold out of here and do all the hard work, then you can take a short cut to Kingdom Come!'

'And take with us the secret whereabouts of a gold mine worth infinitely more than these few cases?' Meredith asked, raising an eyebrow. 'Very well, if you wish it that way.'

Bart looked at his father under his lids, trying to figure what on earth he was talking about. He was careful, however, not to betray that he was mystified. Jane too, sensing something was afoot, kept her face straight, watching.

'Gold mine?' Bannock repeated. '*What* gold mine?'

Meredith contemplated him, smiling faintly. 'Do I have to tell you – a Westerner born – that there are gold mines throughout Arizona which have been abandoned by weary prospectors? That there are fabulous seams known only to the Aztecs themselves? I was just wondering – since we seem to have lost the battle – if you would be prepared to grant us three our freedom in return for that information and the location of the mine?'

Bannock hesitated, frowning.

'You ain't got nothin' to lose, Jack,' Sam said quickly, avarice in his voice. 'Make 'em show you where it is, and if they're tryin' to pull somethin' you can still shoot 'em.'

'Yeah, mebbe you got somethin',' Bannock admitted. He was thinking that even if the mine was genuine, he could *still* shoot them.

'There are conditions, however,' Meredith added. 'My son and I do not know the location of this mine – but his wife does. She discovered it only a few days ago and can take us straight to it. Indeed she was intending to do so – only the matter of the stampede and other details held things up a bit.'

Jane lay and wondered but did not speak. She could not fathom in the least what her father-in-law was driving at – and neither could Bart.

'All right, if that's the way of it,' Bannock said. 'I still hold all the aces anyways. Baldy, git that dame on her feet and carry her down to one of the cayuses – and stay beside her to see she don't attempt nothin'. You two mugs git these cases out of here and make it snappy.'

Meredith docked his cigarette on the topmost case of the two remaining, then with Bart's help got the removed crate on to his shoulder. Baldy went over to Jane and dragged her up on to her sound foot.

'Carry her over your shoulder,' Bannock ordered. 'You can keep your gun clear in your other hand if you do that.'

Baldy nodded and raised the girl over one shoulder. She made no resistance in case it might hinder whatever plan Meredith had in mind.

'And make it quick,' Bannock ordered, as Bart, Meredith, and then Baldy – bearing Jane – went down the tunnel. He turned to his remaining henchmen. 'Sam, Mike – help me git these other two cases ready for them two to carry out when they get back.'

In a moment or two, Bart and his father were in the open, Baldy coming up in the rear as they went down the incline for the second time to the horses.

'What in hell is the idea?' Bart demanded, keeping his voice low. 'What's all this gibberish about a gold mine? You're just asking for trouble!'

'Quite the contrary.' Meredith had an unshakeable calm. 'I think I've just pulled what may be considered a master-stroke. The gold mine strategy was simply an expedient to get Jane out of the cave.'

'Some good that does us! This guy

following us with a gun and Bannock up there waiting for us with another gun! We haven't a cat in hell's chance.'

'I wonder, Son – I wonder?'

He and Bart had reached the horses and the crate was heaved up on to the second animal. Jane was deposited on the third, then Baldy stood back with his gun ready for any false moves.

'Keep alert, Bart,' Meredith murmured, as they corded the crate into position. 'At any moment now something should happen which will distract friend Baldy's attention. Leave it to me to deal with him, since I know what's coming!'

Bart nodded, mystified, looking about him in the growing daylight – then suddenly he was convinced that the world had come to an end.

From high up the mountainside there came a mighty explosion. Rocks, earth, smoke, and a flash of blinding flame all belched out of the cave mouth, the echoes hurling back the din. Rocks, dislodged from above by the concussion, clattered down the slope.

Startled, Baldy wheeled and Meredith dived, bringing the man down in one move and pinning him, wrenching his revolver from his hand. Released, Baldy got up again slowly, bewildered.

'What the hell happened?' he gasped.

'Plenty,' Meredith responded, smiling urbanely. 'I fancy, friend Baldy, that your friends have taken the short cut to Kingdom Come which was intended for us. With only you left to deal with I think we may call this little war at an end. If necessary what's left of the bodies of Bannock and – er – Mike and Sam can probably be found in the cave ruins for the authorities to identify.'

'But what *happened?*' Bart insisted, staring above at the dispersing smoke. 'I still don't get it!'

'Perfectly simple, Son. The two topmost crates contained gold – as we know from the task we have had hauling them down here, but the third one contained *gunpowder*. What was in the fourth one, resting on the floor, I don't know. Perhaps gold, perhaps gunpowder, perhaps anything. You will recall that all the Wells-Fargo consignment was stolen. The thieves responsible evidently took gunpowder as well as gold but evidently had not the time to discover the fact. They left their booty and Bannock assumed – as I did at first – that every case contained gold.'

'How did you know that wasn't so?' Jane asked in astonishment.

Meredith smiled faintly. 'When Bannock fired at Bart the bullet smashed through the wood and into the case. A black, granulated substance trickled out. I noticed it at once. It might have been ground coffee, or even tea, but I reasoned that such items would not be likely to be sent by a stage-coach along with the gold, whereas gunpowder – used in mining – very easily might. Dirt had obliterated the warning marks from the crates, so there was no way of knowing.'

'Then that bullet could have exploded the gunpowder?' Bart asked, thinking.

'It could, Son, but thank heaven it did not. Gunpowder explodes at naked fire, but not often from the impact of heat or a bullet. However, I rectified that omission. Once I had managed to arrange for Jane's safety I left my cigarette butt, still smouldering, in the hole the bullet had made, trusting to the dim light that Bannock would not notice my little subterfuge. I had estimated it would take a few minutes for the stub to burn down and then automatically drop into the gun-powder in the case. However, I think Ban-nock must have moved the case in readiness – assisted by Mike and Sam – and so the effect was more rapid. With most gratifying results!'

'I'll be damned!' Bart declared frankly.

'Hardly, Son,' Meredith responded, beaming. 'But no doubt Bannock and his companions will be! And friend Baldy here will doubtless be of interest to the authorities... For ourselves we have nothing to do but get Jane to the doctor and then hand this gold over and obtain whatever reward there may be, together with the reward for taking care of Bannock and his cronies. With that money – not inconsiderable, I fancy – the town can be rebuilt. And if we are still required as mayor and sheriff I don't doubt but what we can fulfil our obligations.'

'There are times, Randle, when I suspect that you are something of a miracle man,' Jane said, making an effort to smile.

Meredith raised his dusty Homburg gracefully and then returned it firmly into position on his semi-bald head.

'You flatter me, Jane. I purely used psychology, and Bannock did everything I wished once he thought he could get more gold – even to sending you to safety... Ah, the sunrise!' he added, glancing towards the vermilion in the east. 'I think our long night has at last been lifted.'

The publishers hope that this book has given you enjoyable reading. Large Print Books are especially designed to be as easy to see and hold as possible. If you wish a complete list of our books please ask at your local library or write directly to:

**Dales Large Print Books**
Magna House, Long Preston,
Skipton, North Yorkshire.
BD23 4ND